USA TODAY BESTSELLING AUTHOR

Dale Mayer

Saul's SWEETHEART

HEROES FOR HIRE

SAUL'S SWEETHEART: HEROES FOR HIRE, BOOK 8
Beverly Dale Mayer
Valley Publishing Ltd.

ISBN-13: 978-1-773360-43-0
Print Edition

Books in This Series:

Carson's Choice: Heroes for Hire, Book 28
Dante's Decision: Heroes for Hire, Book 29
Steven's Solace: Heroes for Hire, Book 30

Boxed Sets and Bundles
https://geni.us/Bundlepage

About This Book

Welcome to Saul's Sweetheart, book 8 in Heroes for Hire, reconnecting readers with the unforgettable men from SEALs of Honor in a new series of action packed, page turning romantic suspense that fans have come to expect from USA TODAY Bestselling author Dale Mayer.

Helping a friend in need is never a wrong move. And Saul knows the value of his friends. When he's called to find Benji's missing brother, Daniel – he's on it.

Only Daniel might be involved in something a lot darker than avoiding his brother's phone calls. At least according to Rebel who's been haunting Daniel's apartment, looking for her missing girlfriend.

When the bodies start showing up, Rebel is terrified her friend will be next…

And that's not something she's going to sit by and allow. No matter if Saul thinks she should. He needs to get out of her way or she'll run right over him. The trouble is, it doesn't take long for her to realize he'd like that – and so would she.

Now if only they could save their friends…before the entire mess blows up and takes them all out.

Sign up to be notified of all Dale's releases here!
https://geni.us/DaleNews

Chapter 1

SAUL KRESCHNER DROVE into the compound, the truck full of supplies. He'd been to Houston to pick up a couple parts that Ice needed for one of the helicopters. As he slowed to a stop and pulled off to the side, he frowned at the rushed activity going on around him. Something was up. He knew two teams headed out today, but that didn't account for the hard looks on various faces. He opened the truck door, hopped out and walked to where Levi talked to Merk.

Levi faced Saul. "Pack up, ready to go in twenty."

Saul nodded. "Going where?"

"West Coast. Not sure past that. Benji, a friend of ours from the old unit, his kid brother has gone missing. The team is heading out to help him."

Saul nodded. "I'll go pack." He raced inside and headed to his room, not hearing anything about Benji's brother until now. He focused on what he knew about Benji. As Levi was legendary, anyone associated with him was notorious. Benji was a little more so than most. The guy was supposedly massive, bigger than Stone. But with that huge baby face of his, he was said to have an angelic smile that could coax the clothes off any woman. Saul had never met Benji in real life; he just knew the man was one hell of a SEAL. That was good enough for Saul.

When one of them needed help, they all stepped up to

answer.

Benji's personal association with Levi and Ice meant everything else would get dropped to help him and his kid brother. Those other security jobs were business, this was about friends and family, which were everything to SEALs. The loved ones of the men they served with were included as well. For SEALs, brotherhood was paramount.

Saul was in the kitchen within fifteen minutes to find Alfred busy packing baskets. He dropped his duffel bag near the breakfast nook. "I guess those are for me, huh?"

Alfred pointed to the muffins and coffee. "You'll be airborne within an hour, so you can grab a snack if you need to, but these are for the other guys."

Saul nodded. "Don't know how you do it, Alfred. Isn't it time you got yourself some full-time help here?"

"Maybe," Alfred said with a half smile. "I have a niece I was thinking of asking. Maybe I'll talk to Levi about it."

"If she's anything like her Uncle Alfred, sounds like she could be a good fit."

"Yes," Alfred said with one bob of his head. "But I'm not sure it'd be fair to her. A lot of unattached males are around here. And, at the rate they are pairing up, she might be seen as available, yet she's not. Not yet."

"Are you afraid she might get in a relationship with one of us or that she might be too late to snatch one of us up?" Saul teased. He knew as well as Alfred did that all the guys here were good solid men.

Alfred chuckled. "The lucky man would be given a treasure, as if from above, and she would be blessed to become a part of this, my extended family. But the … timing may be wrong for her."

Though Saul liked to think any woman would be happy

to be here with him, he wasn't so arrogant as to say that. He was one of the unattached males. Dakota was another. Sierra's brother, Jarrod, had been back and forth many times, visiting. He was still single. At the rate Levi's company expanded its personnel roster, Saul wouldn't be surprised if another half-dozen men joined them.

He retrieved his duffel, grabbed a cup of coffee and two muffins, then headed outside. Dakota was already in the truck. Placing his bag in the back, Saul hopped in. Merk stood nearby, talking to Levi and Ice. Saul could barely hear their conversation.

"We'll connect with the local authorities in San Diego as needed, probably set up our base at one of the usual hotels," Merk said. "I don't want to disturb Richard with this if we don't need to."

"My father is not in town," Ice said to Merk as Saul listened in. "He's at a conference in Geneva. Foster said the house is yours to stay in. I'm sending four men—Saul, Dakota, you, and Stone. But, in case this ends up being something minor, I have a couple other issues for you to look at when you're over there."

Saul frowned. Did Ice just try to make good use of their time out west? Was something else going on? They'd had several California cases lately. He'd been happy to move to Texas after Harrison's case. Saul had done several runs for Levi since, and this would be his first chance to return to California. He'd hoped to visit with his mother, but she was on a cruise this week. Just the two of them were left now. He hated to see her alone so much of the time, although she apparently enjoyed her lifestyle, which included a lot of traveling. They kept in touch via phone calls, so he knew she wasn't missing him.

"What issues?"

"A look at a few new recruits."

As one of the two newest additions to the team, that surprised Saul. But he had to admit Levi was incredibly busy. "If you're looking for more men, I have a couple friends you should consider. One took medical leave, but is since on his feet again – that's Kris. And Theo left just after Saul and I did."

"Good to know. I'll do some research on them both while you're gone. We'll talk when you get back." She smiled. "Maybe you won't have to meet the men in California then. We'll see how the job goes."

Merk walked over, then took one look at Dakota and said, "I'll drive."

Dakota nodded and hopped into the back of the double-cab truck. Saul already knew how this would work. He saw Stone approach. Saul vacated his seat and joined Dakota.

Stone raised an eyebrow. "You didn't have to do that."

Saul shrugged and said with a grin, "We rookies try to show a little bit of respect for our elders."

Stone chuckled. "Glad to see you know your place."

Once on the move, Stone handed out several sheets of paper. "This is what we know. And it's damn little. Benji got a phone call from his brother at 11:00 p.m. two nights ago. Everything appeared normal, and they arranged to meet for breakfast the next morning. When Benji arrived, his brother was a no-show. He called, but got no answer. He returned to his brother's apartment, again, no answer. He'd either skipped breakfast or just forgot. Benji didn't think anything of it. He continued to call, text, and stop by the apartment at the end of the day. Finally he broke in, only to find it completely empty. Totally cleaned out, ready to rent to somebody else. As far as Benji understood, his brother had been there twenty-four hours earlier. Benji has seen his brother off and on in the months prior and had even been at the apartment. All had been normal. He's called the police, reported his brother as missing and the cops brought in forensics. No word as to any evidence they may have found at this time."

Saul stared at him. "Do we know for sure it was his brother who called him?"

Stone smiled. "Good question. Benji believes it was. Daniel's number came up on his cell phone. But was it Daniel speaking?" Stone shrugged. "We have to figure that one out."

"Is Benji in trouble?"

"He's with the brass right now. He should get through this without any trouble, and he's to ship out today for another mission. To stay in and to keep his nose clean, he needs to do that mission. So he called in the next best thing, which is us."

"That works. So who is his brother?" Saul asked. "What does he do for a living? And why the hell would he book it and leave Benji without telling him anything about it?"

Dakota, sitting beside Saul, asked, "What's the basics? Younger brother, older brother, how old, same parents or stepbrother? What do we know?" He looked through the pages he held in his hands. "All that's missing on these sheets."

Saul studied the couple pages clipped together in his hands. "He's a programmer?"

"Yes," Merk said. "And that always makes our job much harder."

Saul nodded. If Daniel was a good programmer, could

he hide his tracks? "So we need to determine if he left on his own, felt it was his only option, or was kidnapped."

"Or murdered," Merk said quietly. "I've known Benji since we were kids. That brother of his always skirted the outside fringes of the law. He seemed to straighten up but then occasionally took a dip on the wrong side again."

"So it could be as simple as a drug deal gone wrong, should the brother be into that, or having an affair with the wrong married woman."

"And both of those have been issues in Daniel's past," Stone said. "We've known Benji for a long time. Because of that, all his family members tend to become part of our group in some way or another."

"Daniel, the opposite of Benji, used to laugh at him for all his patriotism. Daniel is the kind of guy who wouldn't have made it into the military. He's completely undisciplined, a bit of a wild card, always thumbing his nose at authority and doesn't believe the rules apply to him," Merk added.

"Okay, so what's one of the good things about this guy?" Dakota asked.

"He's a good father," Merk admitted. "He has a four-year-old. Although Daniel's no longer living with the mother, he pays child support and is very heavily involved in the little boy's life. He visits on alternate weekends as well as picks up and takes him to school on the days his mother can't. They play soccer together. He's got him in Little League baseball."

"Interesting. So, walking on the wild side, but, when it came down to it, he bellied up and stepped up to be a man." Saul always found it interesting how the bad boys ended up not being so bad when it came to looking after their own.

"That's good to know." He went through the few stats they had. "He got a DUI?"

"Yes, ten years ago. So far we have no leads on what could have happened now," Merk added. They were almost at the airport.

Saul studied the terrain outside and murmured, "Does Benji have any idea where his brother would've gone to ground or why?"

"All Benji knows is somewhere between making plans for breakfast and meeting for it, his brother either bolted or was removed against his will."

That brought up another question. "Okay, I don't know Benji as well as you guys do. He's got some notoriety within the military, but what I need to know is, is he blind to his brother's faults?"

Merk shook his head. "Benji is very basic. He's hauled his brother's sorry ass out of the ditch more times than he cares to admit. But, when his nephew, Judson was born, he was proud to see his brother stepping up to be a good father. So Benji understands exactly who and what his brother is."

"And does he know if his brother is hooked up in any shady drug deals or has borrowed money from the wrong person?"

"No. Benji says their relationship was getting stronger these last few months, and he thought maybe Daniel was settling down. Daniel never mentioned any trouble, never showed any stress or sign he was up against something he couldn't handle. He was always cocksure and arrogant. But lately he'd been less so, and happier."

Saul slouched against the seat and thought about that. Often *happier* meant *settled in a relationship*. "He's no longer with the mother of his child. Does he have a new girlfriend?"

"Benji thought Daniel was seeing someone after the breakup with Judson's mom, but that didn't last. Benji doesn't know if there was anyone recently, but if someone has any idea what might be going on in Daniel's life, it would be a girlfriend for sure."

"And then potentially it's not Daniel who did something wrong, but, just by association, this woman may have an ex in her life who won't tolerate any competition."

Merk made a left turn, taking them around to the long-term airport parking. "This could end up messy. Ice is already checking out all the local morgues for any John Does, just in case."

"Such an ugly thought." Saul said as Merk parked the car. Saul hopped out, grabbed his duffel bag, threw it over his shoulder and walked around to the front of the truck where the rest of the men had converged.

An hour later they were on a plane heading west. Saul had done this trip many times. He didn't object to any kind of traveling. He liked to use the time to sort through some hypotheses.

He leaned across the aisle. "Merk, do we know anything about Benji's parents?"

Merk nodded. "Both retired, doing a lot of RVing right now, traveling across the country. They sold their house, gave away all their extra belongings and live in their motor home."

"Could Daniel be staying with them?"

Merk shook his head. "No, that's not in the cards."

Saul straightened in his seat and reached into his bag, pulling out a notepad. He was a great listmaker. He wrote down the possibilities as they flowed through his mind, adding options and action steps they needed to take. One—

find any girlfriends. Two—check with neighbors, see what activity they noticed at the apartment over the last few weeks. Three—check brother's place of employment. When was he last at work? What was his mood and attitude? Did anybody know where he'd gone? Where else might he be living? Four—find his vehicle. Five—check the banks and credit cards. He put an asterisk beside the last one. Ice could do that; probably already had.

"How long we got allotted for this?"

"Two days to start, to see what information comes to light," Merk said. "Longer—as long as necessary—up to a point."

Saul nodded. Anything for friends, but still their available time had limits. If they were doing something effective, that was no problem. The minute it stopped being productive use of their time, then there was a problem.

He kept writing down his thoughts, looking at the options, and all the things that could've gone wrong. When his brain calmed, he set aside his pen and stared past Stone out the small window of the plane. That made him think, what about Daniel booking a flight? Saul quickly picked up his pen and wrote a note to check if Daniel's passport had been used, just in case Daniel made a cash purchase of airline tickets, because then the transaction wouldn't show up when Ice ran his credit cards. Maybe he'd left the country.

Merk held out a hand. "May I see that?"

Saul looked at him. "It's just random thoughts."

"Still, I'd like to see it, please."

Saul handed over his list.

Merk read a couple of the top items out loud.

"Don't know how you can read my chicken scratches."

"No problem."

Saul shrugged and settled back. He hadn't meant anybody to read it. They were just notes for himself.

When Merk got to the bottom and returned his notepad, he said, "Well done."

REBEL MATHESON SLIPPED around the corner of the building, her breath catching in the back of her throat. Four men approached Daniel Longmire's apartment complex. Strangers. Big tough badass-looking brutes. She had trouble maintaining 110 pounds when soaking wet. The last thing she wanted was to confront any of those men. But she'd been in tough spots before. Lots of them. It usually took luck and brains to get out of them. She had a black belt in karate, but some things even that wouldn't solve. Still, this was the first interesting thing to show up in the last couple days. Daniel's brother, Benji, had been by a few times, but she'd avoided talking to him after the first time. Did he realize the serious trouble his brother was in right now? You could stick your head in the sand and ignore situations for only so long.

She waited until she thought it was safe, then peeked around the corner. One of the men—Icelandic, tall, broad-shouldered, wearing a T-shirt that hid none of the well-built muscles underneath—stared in her direction. She withdrew quickly, spun and bolted in the opposite direction. She raced around to the rear of the apartment building, deliberately avoiding her car, and ducked between several vehicles. She didn't know what the hell was wrong, but she'd learned to listen to her instincts a long time ago. Something in the man's gaze said, if he ever caught her, he wouldn't let her go without an explanation. And she couldn't give a good one.

Too much deceit and lies were happening right now.

She didn't know who those four guys were or who they worked for, but that one tank of a guy looked like the muscle. Yet the blond guy she had shared a quick gaze with, so far, by the intelligence she saw in his eyes, she guessed he had an analytical mind. She just wasn't sure whether they were good or bad guys at this point.

She debated rolling under the truck beside her—the only way she could nearly disappear. Even then, the blond guy looked like the kind who would know to check if she were hiding there. She finally stood, after ten long minutes, and popped her head up to look cautiously around. When she saw no sign of anybody, she breathed a heavy sigh of relief. Then turned to slip away between the two vehicles.

And came up hard against a big chest. Instantly she knew who it was. She tried to evade him, only to have hands come down around her arms. Just as she went to kick him in the shin, she was spun sideways and pinned against the vehicle. His grip made sure she couldn't possibly get away, yet was also gentle.

"Saul? Find anything?"

"A woman, hiding around the corner, watching us from up front, but bolted when she saw me," he told the man behind him. "Not certain who she is, but I'm pretty damn sure she's keeping an eye on the building."

A man, almost the same size as Benji, said, "Bring her over here."

Slowly, reluctantly, she was walked over to where the other three stood. She frowned at them. Attitude wasn't much of a weapon, but it was about all she had right now. She'd been known to wield it with such finesse that even her mother stopped arguing with her. "Do you always go around attacking people?" she asked them in general.

"Nobody attacked you," one of the others said gently. "But, if you're involved in the disappearance of Daniel Longmire, then that's an entirely different story. We'll be taking you to the police station to discuss it in greater detail."

She could feel the panic flooding her. "I had nothing to do with his disappearance."

"Interesting. So you know Daniel then?" asked the man behind her.

She shrugged off his hold and turned to glare at him. "Yes, but not well. And I wouldn't want to any better. The man's a piece of shit, and, if someone ran him over and tossed him in a ditch, I'd be okay with that."

Chapter 2

IF THESE MEN were Daniel's friends, her comment would hardly win her any brownie points. She took a deep breath. "I need to find his ex-girlfriend, my best friend. She was at Daniel's ten days ago, yet no sign of her since."

"No sign of her in what way?" A dark-haired man stood in front of them with his arms over his chest. "As in she completely disappeared?"

"Exactly. She didn't show up for work, and her mother hasn't heard from her, and she didn't call me. We talk every day, as does she and her mom. She went to Daniel's two Fridays ago. They had a huge fight. She called to tell me she was leaving Daniel's apartment, that she'd phone me when she got home and we could talk later. She never called. I don't think she made it home. I phoned the cops and filed a missing person's report, and there's still been no sign of her. I know it has something to do with Daniel. I just want to find Tammy."

"Did you see Daniel this last week?"

She turned to answer the man who had grabbed her. "I haven't seen him since early last week."

"Three days ago, last Friday night, Daniel spoke with his brother, Benji. Saturday they had plans to meet for breakfast. Daniel didn't show. Today's Monday. There's been no sign of Daniel recently."

She nodded. "I got that much from Benji. This has been really hard on him. I've been dealing with this for over a week now, and still nobody's come forward to help me."

"What about the cops?" the tall dude asked with a hint of a French accent. "Surely they followed up."

She shrugged. "They haven't found anything. I believe they spoke to Daniel too. As far as I'm concerned, he probably did something to Tammy, packed up and got the hell out of here so he wouldn't get caught."

The four men exchanged hard glances.

"How well do you know Daniel?" she asked the group.

The men shook their heads, but the blond spoke to her. "Merk knows him, but the rest of us have never met him. Benji is our friend, so we're trying to find his brother."

She snorted. "When you find Daniel, I want to know what the hell he did to Tammy."

The tank stepped forward and held out his hand. "I'm Stone. The four of us work for Legendary Security out of Texas. We meant it when we said we're here to help Benji. So any information you can give us about Daniel will help us find him sooner, and the sooner we can ask him questions about Tammy's disappearance."

Rebel hesitated. She wanted to trust him, but she'd met way too many hulking men who weren't good guys, and four of them were with her right now, including the one standing to her side. She didn't like how he had snuck so quietly behind her to catch her. "I'm Rebel," she said in a low voice. "And you guys as a group are very intimidating." Yet she thrust up her chin and glared at the tank, the biggest guy of them all.

The big man smiled at her and said, "But inside we're just teddy bears."

She narrowed her gaze at him and snickered. "Right."

The others introduced themselves, and she figured out the man who had caught her was Saul. Two were dark-haired. The man with the accent was Merk, and the taller dark-haired guy was Dakota. "I'd love to get into his apartment and see if any of Tammy's belongings are still there."

"What would that tell you?" Saul asked.

She shoved her hands into her pockets and shrugged. "I don't know. But if we don't start looking, even more time passes without us finding anything, so the less chance we have of locating my friend, and that scares the crap out of me. Tammy is lovely. She wouldn't hurt anybody."

"And yet, she was with somebody like Daniel?"

At that Rebel shook her head. "They were together for a couple months. She broke it off about a year ago. Then maybe a month ago, he contacted her again. I told her to stay the hell away from him as Daniel was just bad news for her."

"Why do you say that?"

"Because a year ago he was living with the mother of his child," she snapped. "Yet persuading another woman that he was single, free, and available." Rebel shook her head. "Tammy doesn't need a lying rat like that."

"That's part of the issue for us since Daniel has not contacted his son, the mother of his child, or his brother either."

At that she frowned. "Is Daniel in contact with his son normally?"

Saul nodded. "All the information we have says he's a very involved father."

She snorted. "That would be the first good thing I've heard about him."

Merk spoke up. "We also understand his apartment is completely empty. Furniture and personal belongings gone. It's been scrubbed from top to bottom."

She stared at him with a gasp. "What?"

"While watching this building for the past several days, you didn't see any moving vans or perhaps furniture coming and going?" Merk asked. "No sign of Daniel packing up and getting out of here?"

"It was the end of the month, a normal time to move in or to out, so residents have been coming and going. I took this last week off to find Tammy," she confessed. "A couple people were moving …" She pressed her lips into a tight thin line. "I haven't seen Daniel though."

"Have you ever been in Daniel's apartment?" Saul asked.

She shook her head. "No, I haven't, so I don't know what it would normally look like." She pulled her phone from her pocket and brought up an image. "This is Tammy." She passed it around for the men to look at. "She's twenty-eight. She's my height, red hair, has lots of freckles with a bouncy personality, tiny, and very smart."

"What did she do?" Stone asked.

"Computers. She worked with Daniel."

"What company was it?" Merk asked.

She named the big telecom company that she, Tammy, and Daniel all worked at. "I'm in the marketing department. Tammy was in programming."

"Did she mention any irregularities there or that she was worried about other coworkers?" Merk asked. "Anybody bothering her? Anybody have any reason to hate her?"

The questions came at her so fast that she struggled to answer. "No, she was happy at work. She didn't say anything as far as I know. Nobody hated her. She's beautiful inside and out." Rebel shook her head. "She's unlike me in a lot of ways. I can be a bitch. Where she would be all sweetness, I'd be the lemon punch. If she sees a puppy running loose, she'll pick it up and bring it home, and I'd be the kind of person who would say the owner probably beat it, and we should take it to a shelter to see if it's injured. She saw sunshine, whereas I would always see the clouds."

As her anger dissipated, her voice thickened with tears. She reached up and pinched the bridge of her nose, getting control of herself. "I don't know what the hell happened to Daniel, and I don't have a clue what he did to Tammy. But two people disappearing who are that closely connected—at work and socially too—can't be a coincidence. They have to be related."

The men nodded. "In that case, you stay with us," Merk said. "We'll find out more if we stick together."

She stared, assessing them again. "I have an apartment. It's not very big, but it's mine. I'm not going anywhere with you guys."

Saul spoke for the first time in a while. "How about to a nice public restaurant for a meal or at least coffee? And we can talk."

On cue her stomach growled. She frowned.

Saul asked, "When did you last eat?"

She wrapped her arms around herself and shook her head. "How am I supposed to eat when, for all I know, Tammy's injured and hasn't eaten for a week?"

"It's a great sentiment," Saul said, "but, if you don't look after yourself, you can't look after Tammy when we find her."

Maybe she was swayed by the conviction in his voice that they would find her… Maybe the deciding factor was that these men looked like they could handle whatever life threw at them, or maybe she was just so damn desperate to have someone care that she believed them capable of getting to the bottom of this nightmare. She knew she couldn't do it alone. She was silent for a long moment and then nodded. "Let's find a quiet place where I can grab some food and coffee, and I'll fill you in on what I do know."

IT NEVER CEASED to amaze Saul how a simple-enough case could blow into something so much bigger. It often happened when he was out on missions and especially since he had started working for Levi. It always seemed to be the same. They had come to look for Daniel, but now they found a woman missing too.

Rebel had brought up another possibility they hadn't considered. Maybe Daniel had lost his temper and done something to Tammy. What if he'd killed this poor woman, then realized he would be an immediate suspect and bolted to save his own hide? Setting it up to look like he just disappeared or had been kidnapped, anything he could do to erase the stain of his guilt from the public eye. Then he could avoid being charged for the crime. At least for a while.

Saul walked toward his Jeep. They were staying at Richard's, and Foster had offered them one of the cars, but, as soon as Saul had arrived, he'd grabbed his own wheels. He hadn't yet had a chance to get his vehicle to Texas.

Everybody got in, keeping Rebel in the middle of the back seat. He went to a popular coffee chain that served food and pulled into the rear parking lot.

They went in and sat around a table in the back corner. After everybody had ordered food and coffee had been delivered, Rebel said, "Tammy's relationship with Daniel started about fifteen months ago. He pursued her at work. She was initially flattered, thinking he was the best thing since sliced bread." Her voice belied her inherent distrust, as if she couldn't believe her friend had fallen for Daniel's used-car-salesman's schmooze.

"But it didn't last. Doesn't take long for the shiny to become tarnished, and she realized he was getting too close to her—to her work. She hung on for a little bit, figuring out what he was up to. And then got in trouble herself when some errors were made through her login. She'd been blamed, even though she had protested. She managed to squeak through that with her job intact, but quickly changed all her passwords and then set about hunting down who did what and used her to do it. Because she was very meticulous with her coding, she also knew other coders' work. She told me how she thought Daniel was the culprit. And that was the reason he'd been acting nice to her. What she didn't know was why he was doing it. It was the kind of prank he loved though."

She shook her head. "Tammy wouldn't have anything to do with him for quite a while after that, and she made a point of changing her login every day before she left the office. Everything non-sequential, nothing anybody could hack easily. Of course, programs are always out there that can, but she had security set up to ensure it wouldn't be easy. Plus, other people were getting into trouble when the same thing happened to them. She said, since she'd been the first one blamed, nobody had believed her at the time. But with three different employees saying somebody hacked their passwords and had adjusted codes, making it look like they'd been the ones doing the sloppy work, the company set up new security. And all those issues stopped."

She glanced over the men. "To me that meant the person who'd been doing the hacking, changing the coding, was inside the company. He had to know that the security had been upped and that, if he did anything else, they would know who it was."

A couple men nodded, and Stone asked, "Did the hackers continue to try to get in?"

She shrugged. "I don't know all the ins and outs of programming, but the hacking stopped."

"What possible reason would there be for making errors in her code?" Merk asked.

"Tammy thought, at the time, it was because they'd been fighting, and he wanted her fired." Rebel stared at her hands. "He was like that back then. Very small-minded, looking for revenge. Tammy says he's changed, but I doubt it. As to whether he'd been the one hacking all the others in the office?" She raised her eyebrows, tilted her head. "I don't know why he would've."

"Unless it was just that he could?" Saul asked. "Maybe he had problems with those people at work?"

"Who knows?" She shrugged. "Anyway, Tammy didn't have a whole lot to do with him after that. She kept her distance at work and never saw him socially. About a month ago he stopped by her desk, all friendly again. He brought her fresh flowers, telling her how sorry he was, that he had taken the last year to get his shit together. He'd separated from his ex-girlfriend, was seeing his son all the time, and he was a different man."

"Tammy believed him?" Saul asked.

"No, not at first. But he worked on her daily. She started to wonder if maybe he *had* changed. They went to a movie, spent some time in the park, just little test-the-water type of dates. She was hesitant to go much further than that."

"Were they in a relationship before she disappeared?" Dakota asked.

"That is one of the odd things. Yes, but not sexually, at least I don't think. He seemed to have straightened up, and she decided she would spend the weekend at his place. She packed an overnight bag. And, yes, we talked about it all week as to whether she should go or not, if she should stay with him. That first night she texted me, saying they had a rip-roaring fight, and she was leaving, and she'd call me when she got home. I waited and waited, but I never heard from her. I went to her place, and she wasn't there. I found no sign she'd made it home. I called her. I texted. I drove past Daniel's place. I searched his building to see if I could find her, but there was just no sign of her."

"How did she get to Daniel's?" Saul asked.

"She took public transit," Rebel said. "She didn't drive, and San Diego is a big city with lots of ways to get around, so she didn't bother to learn."

"So it's possible she was attacked on the way home?" Stone asked.

"It's possible." Rebel stared off in the distance. "I just wish I knew what happened."

"Did you ask Daniel what the fight was about?" Merk asked.

Again she nodded. "I did. He said it wasn't a fight. They just had a slight disagreement. According to him, when she left, she was totally fine. She just wanted to return to her place and think some more. He told me how he didn't want to push her because he wanted her long-term, not just short-term this time."

"Did you believe him?" Saul asked.

"Hell no. The man's a perpetual liar. I can't believe anything that comes out of his mouth."

Saul studied her. So far she appeared to be very forthcoming and open. "When did you go to the police?"

"I ended up there about four o'clock that morning. I told them what had happened. They said they couldn't open a missing person's report for twenty-four hours. But they would see if any attacks were reported anywhere along her route, in case she ended up in the hospital and couldn't give her name or had no ID on her. I phoned the hospitals and checked myself, but found no Jane Does, and nobody with her general description was unidentified." Rebel raised her coffee cup and took a sip. "I asked them to call if any petite redheads were admitted throughout that night."

"What do you think happened to her?" Stone asked.

She eyed him carefully. For such a big man his voice was very gentle. "Of course I'm afraid she's been murdered, but thinking that way would paralyze me. I have to consider that she's okay, that she's running from him and doesn't want to contact anybody she cares about because she's afraid we'll get drawn into the mess with her—or she's incapable of doing so or she's been taken prisoner somehow."

The men stared at her. She had put a lot of serious thought into this, and, for that, Saul was pleased. "Sounds like you're a very good friend." Saul smiled.

"How good a friend am I when she's not home where she belongs?" Rebel snapped. "I'd do anything to bring her back."

Just then their food arrived. Saul waited until she started to eat, recognizing her frustration and temper mixed with hunger as she attacked her food with vigor. "You haven't eaten for a couple days, have you?"

She looked over her fork and shook her head.

He knew the feeling. Nothing like having your whole world fall apart for you to look at life differently. If she wanted to find her friend, she needed to keep her wits about her; otherwise she'd end up in the hospital herself. "What can you tell us about Daniel?" Saul asked as he took a bite of his hash browns.

"At work, he's the guy who does the least and gets most of the recognition. He somehow just shows up in all the brochures and promo because he's got that well-put-together face and smile. But it's kind of smarmy. He's not my kind of guy. I hadn't thought he was Tammy's either. He is extremely persuasive. Very much a ladies' man, very smooth."

"Why isn't he your kind?" Saul realized too late that he shouldn't have asked that question, but it was already out, so he would ignore the men's stares and wait to hear her answer.

"Loyalty, integrity, and honesty. Those will always come above looks, schmoozy mannerisms, and sweet talk for me," she said. "Daniel has none of what matters."

Saul studied her for a long moment. "You really don't like him, do you?"

"I didn't before. Now that I believe he's involved in Tammy's disappearance, I really hate him."

So much truth rang through her voice that he believed her. The trouble was, it was the last thing they needed to hear.

"Did you do anything," Merk asked, "such as threaten him, argue with him, set the cops on him? Anything that would have made him pack up and run?"

She froze, frowned and slowly put down her fork. "On

that note, I don't know. I certainly asked him about her at work, and he said he didn't know what happened after she left his place. I talked to him, told him I'd reported her missing, that he was the last person to see her alive, but Daniel said I was wrong about that. He said that would be whoever had kidnapped her or hurt her, and that hadn't been him because, when she'd left, she'd been alive. I told him I would find out what happened, if it was the last thing I did on this planet, and, if he was responsible, I'd see he paid for it. His response was kind of odd. He said something about hoping that's not the way it turned out, but, if it had to be, then it had to be."

Saul stared at her. "I don't like the sound of that."

"At the time I didn't think anything of it," she confessed. "It just seemed like something he'd say, something to avoid suspicion, and I kind of glossed over it. I even wondered if Tammy would have been so depressed about their relationship failing so soon again that she'd committed suicide, but I dismissed it immediately as I knew she wouldn't have."

"So, when you talked to Daniel at his apartment, when he opened the door, could you see inside?" Stone asked.

She shook her head. "I met him in the lobby. I couldn't go up to his apartment without a reason. And I couldn't have him call the cops on me. I was hoping he would lead me to her, so I've been watching the building ever since." She raised her hands in surrender at their looks. "I know. I know. But what else could I do?"

Saul leaned over and gently gripped her shoulder. "You did what you could. Now just ease back and let us think about this."

She picked up her fork and stared at him again.

He said, "We'll consider other options. Daniel has been missing forty-eight hours. The police have our missing person's report, but, so far, nothing has shown up."

"What about his car?" she asked. "He drives one of those muscle cars, all souped up. Black, I think. Like the one in that long-running TV show."

"*Supernatural?*"

She nodded. "Looks something like that."

"When did you last see it?"

"Months ago, when he arrived at work one day."

"We can get the license plate easily enough." Saul nodded and sent a text to Ice. Her response came back almost immediately, and he glanced at Stone. "Ice will look for it. She's searching for any property he owns, in case he's got a place to go underground."

"Going underground won't help him," Rebel snapped. "Not if he's done something to Tammy. I'll make sure of that."

Chapter 3

A S SOON AS she finished eating, Rebel asked the waitress for a piece of paper. She came back with a small notepad. Rebel thanked her and wrote down all the pertinent information on Tammy. Address, phone number, and her mom's number. That was enough data for these guys to start a search for Tammy for the time being. Then she started in on Daniel. By the time she was done, she was on another cup of coffee, and the men waited for the pieces of paper to come their way.

Rebel put down her pen and said, "That's what I know."

"It's more than we had."

She nodded. "How do I get a hold of you guys if I find out anything else?"

"Let us look for Daniel from now on," Stone said. "We don't want you to get in any trouble. Possibly both disappeared for completely different reasons. But, most likely, Tammy was taken because of her association with Daniel. If that's the case, we don't want you getting involved."

"Trouble?" She frowned at him. "You don't think Daniel did something to Tammy?"

"Not at this point. There are a lot of other options, some of which we have not considered yet."

She crossed her arms over her chest. "That may be, but I still need a way to contact you in the event anything comes up."

Stone glanced at Saul, who pulled out his phone, clicked on his number and held it up for her to see. Rebel grabbed hers and added him to her Contacts.

"And your number is?" Saul asked.

She gave it to him, then stood. "Okay, I've done everything I can here. I'm heading home to get some sleep." When she was halfway across the restaurant, she turned and called back, "Thanks for lunch." She disappeared out the front door.

On the sidewalk, she stopped and considered her options. She had left her vehicle parked behind Daniel's apartment. She had connected with all the neighbors on the same floor as Daniel, except for one. She had hoped they might have seen Daniel.

The manager had been no help. He'd refused to give her any information about Daniel or Tammy. She understood his position, but, if Daniel had moved out or not paid his rent for the next month, the manager could've said something about that. The more she thought about that, the more it upset her. A sure way to hide yourself, thirty days before anybody came looking for you, was to pay your rent, move out ahead of time and get re-established somewhere else. Saul and his buddies might think Daniel was innocent, but she wasn't so sure.

It took her twenty minutes to walk back to the apartment building. She checked that her car was still there; then went back inside, up to Daniel's floor. The crime scene tape was new. And gave her a woozy feeling. If something had happened to Daniel how was she going to find Tammy? She knocked again on the one apartment where she hadn't managed contact with its residents. This time she got a young woman. Rebel asked the same questions, adding one about seeing Daniel moving.

The woman laughed. "Friday night he was taking boxes out of his place."

"Oh, you spoke with him?"

"No, I spoke with his friend, and he said Daniel was pulling a late-night job of it because he was leaving without giving notice."

"You didn't actually see him that night though, did you?"

The woman frowned and stared at her. "I'm not sure I did. I saw boxes of stuff coming out of his apartment, but I only saw his friend."

"Any idea what his friend looked like?" asked a male voice behind her.

She spun around and glared at Saul, standing a little too close to be a stranger and a little too far away to be a lover.

The woman smiled at Saul. "Blond, looked like a surfer." She laughed at that. "Same as almost any male in San Diego. I'd say late twenties, but that's about as close as I can get. He was strong because he carried several big boxes out at a time, and he moved fast."

"Like he was in a hurry?" she asked.

The neighbor nodded. "Yes, that's exactly what it looked like." In the apartment behind her a child screamed. She hurriedly stepped back in. "Sorry, I have to go." And she shut the door.

Rebel turned to look at Saul and found the other men lined up behind him. "Why are you guys here again?"

"Why are you?" Saul laughed.

"I'm here because I'm looking for Tammy."

"And we're here looking for Daniel."

She glared at Saul. "Fine."

"At least now we know somebody saw Daniel's apartment being emptied out on Friday night." Saul looked to Stone. "I suggest we make a quick search. Confirm what Benji saw. See if anything's different."

Stone was already on his way over. He pulled something from his back pocket while she watched. Within seconds Daniel's door was open, crime scene tape hanging off the side. She raced forward. No way they were going in without her. She slipped past Stone and stepped into the apartment first, raising her nose, sniffing. "Bleach."

Silence followed.

She turned to look at them, voicing the horror of what instantly jumped to her mind. "So did Tammy die here or did Daniel?"

Saul shook his head. "Let's not jump to conclusions."

She wrapped her arms around her chest and surveyed the empty space. The apartment was decent with bright lights. As far as she could see, it was completely empty. The kitchen had tile flooring, and the rest of the apartment was laminate throughout. It would probably take forensic testing to prove any blood was left here. She walked to the master bedroom and bathroom. There was nothing left to find, no indication Tammy had even been here or that anybody had met a disastrous fate in this space. She shook her head. "Where the hell has he gone then?"

"We'll find out. Just give us a little bit of time."

"How long have you been looking for him?"

Saul looked at his watch and said, "About three hours. That's when we arrived in California."

Her jaw dropped. "You came to California to find him?"

All four men nodded. "Benji is our friend. We never

leave a friend in need."

"Lucky Benji." She shook her head. "I wish I had had someone to help me find Tammy." She walked in the second bedroom and into the other bathroom. She bent down and opened the doors underneath the sink. It was clean. She pulled them open on the side, hoping maybe something got missed. But even the garbage cans had been dumped. Though the drawers were empty, they hadn't been wiped. "If he left in a hurry he did a good basic cleaning job but didn't get to all the details," she announced.

She got up and walked over to the kitchen where she opened all the cupboards to find anything left behind. People always seemed to leave things in the back of the kitchen drawers. She pulled them out and, sure enough, found some loose paper clips and staples in one drawer. She studied them for a long moment but knew they'd have absolutely nothing to offer in the way of information.

By the time she was done, she was frustrated and angry. "This was my only hope to find a lead to Tammy. I don't even know where to look now," she cried out.

"Any fingerprints of her here won't help because she stayed here," Saul said, turning to look at her. "Have you checked Tammy's apartment to see if there's any sign of Daniel there?"

She nodded. "Yes, as soon as she went missing, and found nothing there."

"But what if Daniel has gone there since then? Knowing she was missing, that left her apartment available to hide in for a day or two."

She liked that idea. "I'll go now and check."

"Wait."

Already on her way to the front door, she spun and

looked at him. "What?"

"I'll come with you," Saul said. "Let them finish what they're doing here. Then they can follow us."

She shrugged. "Whatever. Just don't slow me down." And she raced back into the hallway.

Instead of waiting for the elevator, she took the stairs. Downstairs she burst outside, heading toward her car. Before she could get the driver's door open, Saul was already at the passenger side, waiting for her to unlock it. She shot him a look.

He grinned. "You said, *don't slow you down.*"

He seemed awfully good at sticking close. She was a little worried about having him in her vehicle, but, although he was big and muscled, she didn't feel threatened.

She quickly reversed her car from the parking lot and pulled into traffic.

"We're about ten to fifteen minutes away," she said.

"That's fine." He pulled out his phone and spent the rest of the drive on it, instead of socializing with Rebel.

It was kind of a relief and also an irritant. She kept glancing at him as he sent message after message. "So you're sending a text to your girlfriend that you'll be out of town?"

"Nope. Got no girlfriend. This is all business."

That had been cheeky of her to ask about a girlfriend, but getting his answer made her feel much better. Still, that she'd even asked was a surprise. Just because a gorgeous male sat beside her, it didn't mean he was available in any way, shape or form, or that she was even interested. She had a lot more things on her mind than that. All she had to do was think about what happened to Tammy—who wouldn't listen to her advice about Daniel—to make Rebel want to stop and kick this man out of her car. But there was absolutely no comparison between Daniel and Saul. At least none that she could tell in the couple hours she'd known Saul.

She pulled up in front of Tammy's apartment and hopped out.

Saul got out, looked at the location and the big trees down the street and smiled. "Nice area."

"It is. She's lived here about six years."

She led the way inside and up to the top floor. At the first apartment, she knocked with her ear against the door, but no sound came from inside, so Rebel pulled Tammy's key from her pocket, inserted it and carefully pushed open the door. As she went forward, Saul grabbed her shoulder, placing a finger on her lips. With one eyebrow raised, she stepped back and let him go in first.

SAUL STEPPED FORWARD, listening intently to see if they were alone. He couldn't hear or see anyone, but that didn't mean somebody wasn't hiding within. He stepped into the feminine space and smiled to see the purple rubber duck sitting on the mantel. A lot of personality was in this apartment. He did a quick walk-through, making sure it was all empty. He didn't have any reason to believe there would be an intruder, but, with two people missing, he couldn't be careful enough. He didn't want somebody like Rebel to take a walk and nobody to see her again either.

After his quick search, he came back and nodded. "It looks to be clear."

The other three men came up the hallway as Rebel stepped inside. He motioned at them and said, "It's empty."

They walked in, splitting up in the different parts of the apartment to search. He chose the bedroom, heading straight for the night table. He opened the drawers and pulled out a notebook.

Rebel stood in the doorway. "What are you doing?"

"Looking for answers. Looking for where she might be or who she may be with. Looking for clues to see if she was taken against her will."

"By going through her personal possessions?"

He heard the shocked embarrassment and anger for her friend.

He turned to look at her. "Do you believe she's missing?"

Rebel nodded.

"Then this is what we have to do. So get over your embarrassment, that sense of violation and intrusion, and realize what we're doing will help her, not because I have any voyeuristic wish to read her diary."

She stepped closer. "Sorry. It's just the shock of seeing you head straight for the night table. She always kept her personal stuff there."

"Which is exactly why I am here. Does she have a laptop? What about her cell phone?"

"Her laptop is here. She has a cell phone, but it's going straight to voicemail."

"Can you check the apartment for her phone, maybe call it to see if it's been left behind?"

She pulled out her phone and called. They listened, both tilting their heads to the side to hear better. She got no answer, and no ringing sound could be heard in the apartment.

"That doesn't necessarily mean anything," Saul said. "Her phone battery could be dead." He glanced at Rebel as he rummaged through the night table. "You know if she has a diary, besides this notebook, or an address book?"

She shook her head. "Everything's on her laptop or maybe her tablet."

He nodded. "Where's the tablet?"

Rebel spun around in a slow circle. "I ..." She went to the other night table and checked. Then she went to the dresser, opening the top drawer. "It's not here. I'll look in the living room, but she might have taken it to Daniel's with her. It was just for personal use so I'm not sure it's an issue."

He nodded. He did a quick search of the other night table. Not a whole lot was here. He found a journal, but the last entry was over a year ago. It was interesting reading about Daniel and how angry she was when she found out he was messing with her coding at work. Saul hung on to the diary, went to the closet for a quick examination, then to the dresser. So far nothing was out of the ordinary, nor gave any indication of a struggle, and there was certainly no suicide note. So far it was as if she just got up, walked out and never came back. The closets and dresser were full of clothes.

He headed back to the kitchen, then realized he'd forgotten to check the bathroom. He gave it a quick search but didn't find anything. He walked out to find Stone sitting at the kitchen table with the laptop open and on. "Is there a password on it?"

Stone nodded. "Of course there is. She's in IT. But the password was way too easy."

"What's way too easy?" Rebel asked.

Stone looked up, gave her a glimmer of a smile. "The password." The men turned and looked at him. Stone shrugged. "Too often people use the same one at work and home."

"She used to have complicated ones," Rebel said in defense of her friend. "But then she had a problem a couple years back with her mother who couldn't remember her password to get into her laptop to take care of some banking. Since then, on her personal devices, Tammy stuck with one her mother could remember."

Stone nodded. "I've seen things like that happen before too."

"Anything of interest?"

"Lots of emails back and forth between her and Daniel. They were planning to spend the weekend together. Nothing out of the ordinary, providing this email came from Daniel."

Saul turned at the sudden silence beside him.

Rebel stared at Stone. "Meaning, she could've been led to believe this was her old relationship coming together, only all these emails may not have been coming from Daniel?" She shook her head. "No. That doesn't make any sense. She was with Daniel a lot at work."

"Were you privy to the conversations they had there?" Merk asked.

She shook her head. "No. But she told me how he'd been a lot friendlier."

"Probably not on the same level," Dakota said. "It's possible she was lured somewhere else after leaving Daniel's in a huff."

She plunked down at the kitchen table. "But, if that's the case, how do we find her?"

Saul lifted his gaze. "We can only follow the breadcrumbs. What we find at the end of the pathway, nobody can tell. Keep the faith, and we'll do what we can." He faced Stone. "Can you track the email?"

"Already working on it. It's a sophisticated system, but they are both computer geeks."

"Is it beyond you?"

Stone shot Saul a look. "Talk like that will get you in trouble."

Saul smiled. "Not trying to insult you, just wanted to make sure we don't need to bring in somebody else for it."

"There may not be anything here to find."

"Ice can check her bank activity from two Fridays ago and thereafter. She's already looked into hotels up and down the coast. No evidence she made a reservation though. We'll have to find out from Ice if Tammy's credit cards had any action."

Saul stepped away and called Ice. He explained where they were and what Stone had found.

Ice confirmed, "No bank activity or action on either of her credit cards."

"That's not good."

"It's not necessarily bad either. If I took off, the last thing I'd do is use my cards. It would be too easily traceable. Much better to go with cash and apply for new cards when you got set up in a new location."

"True enough. I can't connect with Benji either."

"Benji is now overseas. He shipped out this afternoon before you landed."

"Explains why he never answered his calls."

"Find out what you can and call me tonight. It'd be nice to have something to report."

"Unfortunately, right now we don't have anything. Daniel's been missing for a couple days, and this woman Tammy has been for a week longer. Her last known whereabouts was at Daniel's apartment with him. However, one of the neighbors at Daniel's place did say she saw somebody taking boxes from Daniel's apartment on Friday night. Apparently he was moving quickly. She did not see anybody else and, when questioned further, couldn't determine if Daniel had been there."

"So it's quite possible somebody went in and cleaned out his apartment to make it look like he'd moved."

"There could be all kinds of reasons for this but, yes, it's been cleaned out. And, as Rebel stated when she walked in, there was a strong smell of bleach."

Ice sighed. "I can check again with the local PD on the case. Maybe they will give us a few details. I did a run on Daniel's car. It was towed from outside his apartment in a no parking zone. I haven't found any property under his name yet. Also no hits on the credit cards. If someone stole them they haven't used them yet."

"Don't tell Benji."

"I won't be telling Benji anything until we get some proof. He's likely to go off half-cocked, tearing the town apart, looking for his brother when he returns stateside."

"Daniel's had a pretty rough life, but he was improving. According to Benji, he had a lot of hope that his brother was turning his life around since his son was born four years ago."

Ice sighed heavily. "Let's hope we find both people soon." Just like that she hung up—in total Ice style.

Chapter 4

S HE'D DONE WHAT she could. She didn't know what else to do. She'd searched Daniel's place. She'd searched Tammy's—twice now—finding it as empty and clean as she always left it. There was no sign of her. Where could she be?

Stone worked on the laptop beside her at a table, while she slumped in Tammy's chair. She'd spent many happy hours here with her friend, laughing and crying, going over all the things that made life so special between friends. She was desperate to get word as to what had happened to her best friend. She brought up her phone and dialed Tammy's number. She glanced up and saw Saul watching her.

"What are they looking for?" she nodded at the two men intent on their computers.

"Other missing persons cases, or kidnappings in the area. They are looking for anything that might link to Daniel and Tammy's disappearances." He pulled out his phone. "I'm searching for pawn shops in the area. On the off chance whoever cleaned out Daniel's apartment might have tried to make a few fast bucks."

"And Dakota?"

He sighed. "Dakota got a hit on a couple Jane Does in the area. He went to check them out personally."

At her cry of shock, he reached across and said, "He's already checked in. Neither were Tammy."

She stared at him wordlessly. None of this had even occurred to her to check out. She pulled out her phone and instinctively hit the redial button. Then winced. "I can't stop trying to contact her. I keep hoping she'll answer."

Sitting beside Stone, Merk had his laptop open too and looked up. "What's the number?" She told him, and he entered it into the laptop.

She watched with interest. "What are you doing?"

"Checking again for the last time that number was used and from where," he said quietly, his fingers busy on the keyboard. "Which was from Daniel's apartment. Two Fridays ago."

"When she called to tell me that she was on her way home." She leaned forward and stared at them—waiting for an answer. "Does that mean she was attacked at his apartment?"

"We don't know that from this data," Saul said quietly. "Only that her phone was last used at Daniel's."

She settled back. "Right. Can you track it?"

Merk shook his head. "No, I can't. Most smartphones can be, but hers is an older one. Either the tracking wasn't installed, has been turned off, or is corrupted."

She nodded. "As far as I'm concerned, everyone should have GPS."

"You can get apps to help as well."

She nodded. They had confirmed something at least. Though not the answers she'd hoped for, it gave credence to the fact Tammy could have been attacked at Daniel's.

Merk looked up at her. "Was she nervous about taking buses?"

Rebel shook her head. "Tammy was a pro at them, but I hated her taking them at night. I wanted to pick her up, but she was so distraught that she wouldn't listen. Daniel should've seen her home safely."

"But, if they were fighting, she probably would've refused his help."

Rebel nodded. "That's true."

"Does she have any other friends she'd have gone to?" Saul asked. "Somebody who might have an apartment she could crash at or another place to just get away to for a bit as she got her head on straight?"

Rebel shook her head. "No, not that I know of." Tammy would have contacted her mother regardless.

"Do you know if Daniel has a storage locker in his apartment building?"

Again she shook her head. "I don't know. Tammy has a small one here in her building. But, after some flooding, she took everything out so the storage areas could be repaired, and never bothered using it afterward."

"Each tenant should have one. But we never thought to check." Saul stood. "I'll check Tammy's, just to make sure. We can't go back into Daniel's apartment as the forensic team is either currently working or has sealed it off."

Rebel nodded. "Fine, I'm coming too."

She walked out of Tammy's apartment with Saul to the elevator and down to the basement. She turned on the lights, showing Saul locker upon locker. Reading the numbers, she quickly led them to the back corner where Tammy's storage area was located. It was empty, as she'd said.

"I'll go see if I can check Daniel's place."

"May I come?" she asked.

He shook his head. "You stay here, in case Tammy turns up, or the guys find out something and need further information from you." He pulled out his phone and called

Merk, still upstairs in Tammy's apartment. "I'm heading to Daniel's building to check out his storage area. Tammy's is empty. I'm sending Rebel back to you guys."

His phone at his ear, he groaned and glanced at Rebel. "She can come with me if you think that's better." Saul listened, then said, "Okay, fine. Be back in half an hour or so."

As he put away his phone, she grinned. "So it's okay? I can come?"

He nodded. "I can't say it's the best decision, but let's go."

With that, she raced off ahead of Saul. "Then we'll go in my car as I know the way."

WHILE SITTING IN the passenger seat of Rebel's car while she drove, Saul sent Merk a text, asking,

Why take her with me?

To keep her close. She seems most open with you. She's the only one who has any idea what's happened.

Meaning, she could be lying? Or withholding something?

I doubt it. Her fear for her friend is real. Her hatred for Daniel is just as real. Yet she might remember something, something inconsequential to her.

Fine. Be back soon.

Watch your back.

Saul put away his phone, thinking about Merk's words.

Was Rebel in danger? Were they all in danger? If somebody had killed Daniel in his own apartment, would they maintain watch on it? Then take steps to eliminate any further threats? When you commit murder once, the second time is that much easier.

The one person who had been consistently at that location in recent days was Rebel.

She pulled into the back of Daniel's building again. The two of them walked around to the front, waited for somebody to come out so they could enter. He had another option for getting in, but he didn't want to break in if he didn't have to. However, they didn't have to wait long as a neighbor walked out and held the door for them and carried on without even noticing.

Up at Daniel's, Saul unlocked the door, using his lock pick, and stepped inside for a quick look around to see if anybody had been there since the last time Saul was here. It appeared the same overall. When he took a closer look, he found strands of hair, one on the inside at the front door and one farther inside the apartment—Merk's work. The guys all had personal favorite traps to set to ensure no one had entered a room while they were gone without their knowledge. This had all the hallmarks of Merk. The first Saul had dislodged when he opened the door, and the second was still intact. Feeling better that the place was still deserted, he turned and told Rebel, "Let's go to the lockers."

Downstairs, he checked out the various hallways, dividing large open lockers. The apartment block was huge, and one was allotted for each apartment.

He counted down the numbers until he came to Daniel's. He stopped in front of it and stared. It was full. As in seriously full. He smiled and whispered, "Bingo." He double checked the number on the outside of the unit to confirm it corresponded to Daniel's, then dialed Merk. "The locker is full from where I'm standing, but Rebel can't confirm the contents are his though."

"Or it could be somebody else's?" Merk asked. "Why would someone so meticulously clean out Daniel's apartment, then leave behind a packed storage locker? Probably didn't know he had it. Can you see what kinds of items are in there?"

"Lots of moving-size boxes, contents unknown. A couple snowboards and a bike."

"Best guess for the owner of those possessions?"

"Daniel's. There is a padlock on the fencelike gate to the storage area."

"You might need clearance before going in. Give me five."

"Good enough." He turned to see Rebel staring at the locker.

"It's full," she said in surprise. "Why wouldn't Daniel have moved it all?"

"Remember, he's not the one who cleaned out his apartment," Saul said brusquely. "I'm leaning toward something happening to Daniel, and whoever cleaned out his place just made it look like Daniel took off and yet, wasn't aware of the storage locker area down here."

She turned and stared. "But, if that's the case, what happened to Tammy?"

He shot her a grim look. "I don't know yet." His gaze returned to the storage locker. He peered through the mesh door to see what was inside, but it was too dark. It could be boxes of personal belongings, or important things, but it would take hours to go through it all, and that was if they could get into it.

His phone rang once more. "Good enough," he said. He put away his cell, pulled out his lock pick again and worked on the padlock. "We don't need clearance for this. Benji's name is on the lease and gave us permission. If we find anything we're to let Detective Wilson know."

The light was crappy back here, so he had to go by feel when working on the lock. It took him about thirty seconds longer than it should have. Swearing to himself nonetheless, it popped open when the final click engaged. He removed the padlock and opened the door. A light switch was just inside. He flipped it, and a hanging bulb threw an eerie glow over the contents. He went to the first box and opened it, full of winter clothes, sweaters, and jackets. He closed the top flaps and went after another box.

He repeated the process for a couple more, but the next one yielded gold.

"Looks like income tax returns." He opened the box, scanned the top document within the first packet and confirmed it was Daniel's. "Well, that's a start. But, if Daniel was involved in any way with the staging of his empty apartment, the fact that he didn't also dispose of everything in this locker is suspicious."

"Or he had to leave too fast. Plus, he has a month to come back and get this stuff."

He turned to look at her. "You think he's guilty, don't you?"

"I don't know that for sure. You guys have given me moments of doubt. But he's the closest link I have to finding Tammy," she said very quietly. "If he didn't do it, I don't know where else to look."

He understood she was loathe to let go of a suspect, but

she needed to start looking in another corner. A lot of other options were under consideration still. The thing was, without bodies, there could be no closure and often no answers.

Saul's phone rang again. He checked the Caller ID. *Ice.* "Yes, we're in the locker, but I'm not finding anything relevant yet. Did you get anywhere with Daniel's company?"

"Yes, he had asked for time off. He left on a Tuesday and was due back today, but didn't show."

"Nobody at work has seen him since a week ago?"

"No. His coworkers didn't know anything. They figured he was sick. He had not been in the best shape the previous week, so, when he asked for time off, the boss just assumed Daniel was struggling. He didn't give a reason other than the fact he wasn't feeling well."

"Interesting. Did he have any friends we need to talk to at work? Anybody who would know more?"

"Yeah, Tammy." Ice gave a short laugh. "The boss said he'd come close to firing Daniel several times over the last year. Tammy had submitted a complaint against Daniel at one point as well. I spoke to the head of HR, Roger Ginrod. He had no new information on Tammy. He understood the police had opened a missing person's file on her, and, until I brought that up, he hadn't considered Daniel's disappearance questionable at all."

"Even when Daniel didn't show up for work today?"

"Yes, but that's not unusual for Daniel. Plus, no one noticed as his supervisor was scheduled to be in meetings all day."

"So we now have two missing persons from the same office. Yet somebody answered Daniel's phone, potentially Daniel himself, to keep his brother happy."

"Yes, which means it's likely somebody close enough to Daniel knows his brother's a SEAL and would raise shit if something happened to his kid brother."

"Yes, that's quite possible."

"Can you access the security cameras on the apartment building?" he asked Ice.

"We went through proper channels and asked the police. They've refused. It's an ongoing investigation and they aren't willing to share."

"So we are bypassing that, right?" Saul asked with a wince. "I know perfectly well we can. It's just how far across the line are we willing to go?"

"Give me another hour to work my way through this."

He hung up, knowing perfectly well she would find a way around the legal route if she had no other option. But, in the meantime, it would be nice to know the last time Daniel left this property. Saul turned to Rebel to explain. "They tried to get legal access to the security cameras in the building."

"The police said they would check the video cameras here as well," Rebel said. She pulled out her wallet and retrieved a business card. "Have Ice contact this man. He's a detective on Tammy's case."

While she watched, Saul sent the information to Ice in a quick text. "Maybe we'll get some action here after all."

"I hope so. Nothing makes sense to date."

They hadn't gotten more than a few feet away when Ice called back. "Security cameras were down the entire weekend Tammy was there, and the cops suspect Daniel hacked into the system. The detective did say they are treating Tammy's disappearance as a potential kidnapping/murder. But, of course, until her body shows up, or the bad guys make contact, nobody knows what happened for sure."

"Will he work with us?" Saul asked.

"He appeared to be happy to take any information we had to offer. He understood you guys were there looking for Daniel, and that your cases have collided. I've told him that you will contact him sometime in the next hour. I didn't tell him about the storage locker, so, when you call, it will give you something to share."

"Does he know we've been inside the apartment?"

"You're entitled. Benji gave you permission. You have full rights to go in and check."

"Good." Saul hung up and smiled. "At least now we have the law working on our side too."

Chapter 5

B Y THE TIME they walked back outside, frustration and fatigue rolled in waves through Rebel's head. She just wanted this over. But she didn't want it to end with a dead body—not even Daniel's. She wanted her friend back home safe and sound with her bright smile and shiny light-blue eyes in what had often been a dark and dreary world for Rebel. Why was it always the nice people who got hurt? Tammy went out of her way to even help spiders. Like, who did that?

Rebel leaned against the hood of her car and rubbed her temple. Something must have been left behind by whomever did this to her.

"You may have to accept the fact she was accosted on the way home. She could have been attacked at any number of places and not even related to Daniel's disappearance." Saul's voice was low.

"I don't want to accept anything other than her being home safe and sound," Rebel murmured. "But I'm also very aware not all dreams come true. The fact that it's been ten days now terrifies me."

Saul nodded. He leaned against the car hood beside her. "The police should've checked the city traffic cams on the route between Daniel's and her home. It's possible they can find her somewhere on her journey."

"I don't know if they did that. Not even sure they went through Daniel's apartment's video cameras."

"The detective told Ice that the cameras were down. And that, of course, is suspicious."

Rebel nodded. "This is a nice apartment, but the security isn't superhigh. Until somebody checked the footage, they wouldn't know it was down, right?"

He nodded. "Only the high-end apartments have security guards monitoring the comings and goings of their patrons."

"Was the security itself down, or were the video cameras destroyed?"

He shook his head. "I have no idea."

"Big difference. One could've been physical damage, and the other could be IT hacking." She turned and added, "Why no outside security cameras?"

"There is one." He pointed to a camera attached to the light over the parking lot. "I don't know if anybody checked that one or not." He pulled out his phone and sent a text to Ice. When he was done, he returned his phone to his pocket. "What will you do now?"

She turned to look at him. "I can't believe I've only known you for a few hours," she muttered, not answering his question. "It seems like I've known you for years."

He gave her a gentle smile. "Times of stress and upset like this shorten the initial acclimation period when meeting and getting to know people. There is just no time to spend on the social niceties. And often you'll see somebody for a full year, like a neighbor, but you won't have spoken more than a couple dozen words in that time. But it feels like you know them. In our case we just get to the nitty-gritty right away."

She smiled. "Benji must be nice for you guys to pull out all the stops to help him like thisHe showed up at the office to take Daniel to lunch but don't know Benji otherwise."

"He's an awesome guy. He works hard, fighting for our country. If there's anything we can do to keep his family safe, then we'll do it."

She studied Saul for a long moment. "That's very patriotic and very emphatic. Why didn't you join the military if you feel that way?"

"I was in the military—in a unit similar to Benji's. I'm out now. And I'm doing what I can in the private sector."

"Oh." Suddenly she felt a whole lot better being around him. "I hadn't considered it from that perspective."

"A lot of people don't. While Benji's off fighting for us, he can't be here fighting for his brother. That's where we step in."

"Nice. I want to believe Daniel changed over the last year, but I still have my doubts. He broke Tammy's heart the first time. I was shocked when she opened that door again. She said he was so sincere and so different, but I just didn't believe it."

Feeling hot tears burn her eyes, she wiped them away and cleared her throat. The last thing she wanted was to be the weeping, crying, weak woman here. "I just don't know what to do anymore. I've taken the bus from Daniel's to Tammy's apartment and back several times, looking for any place where she might've gotten off, looking for any reason why somebody would've tried to take her. I've walked part of those streets looking at every alleyway. I can't find any trace of her."

He reached out and gripped her shoulder. "I'm so sorry. Unfortunately we often don't get answers for years and years and sometimes never. But that doesn't mean we give up hope."

She stared at the pavement. "I've got hope. But I'm starting to lose faith."

By agreement they drove back to Tammy's apartment, where Merk, Stone and Dakota remained camped out, tied to their computers. As Rebel and Saul walked into the kitchen, an air of excitement surrounded the place. "What's new? What's happened?"

"Benji left his phone with Ice to see if she could trace his last call to Daniel. Benji picked up another one for his own purposes while he's overseas," Stone said.

And Merk continued, "She just intercepted a text message from Daniel."

"What did it say?" Saul demanded.

"*Help.*"

Not what Saul expected at all. "Did we get a location from the text?"

Stone nodded. "In a rough part of town. Down by the docks."

"Interesting," Saul said.

"So we're heading there now?" Rebel asked, heading toward the front door again.

"Almost," Merk said, nodding his head toward Stone as his fingers flew over the keyboard. "Waiting to see if we can pinpoint it a little closer."

"Got it," Stone announced. He spun the laptop around to show a beeping marker on the map.

Saul looked closer. He knew the area. This was a bad street. He turned and headed for the front door. "Let's go."

"Was there any mention of Tammy?"

Dakota looked at Rebel and shook his head. "I'm sorry.

Nothing other than *I'm in trouble. Help.*"

Biting her lower lip, she nodded. "I'll go with Saul."

The men stood, shaking their heads. "No way," Stone said.

Saul added, "I'll let you know as soon as we find anything."

She glared at them. "I have to find out what happened to Tammy."

"And we'll do what we can to find her. But we must get Daniel first. That is our priority. We've tracked him down. If he can help us find Tammy, even better. But we have to get him."

"Maybe Tammy's with him."

"Then we'll rescue both."

She chewed on her bottom lip and glared at them, then finally nodded. But she would follow them anyway.

The men disappeared out the front door. She was left alone in Tammy's kitchen. She quickly locked up her friend's apartment and raced to her own vehicle. They wouldn't know if she was heading home or not, but she'd rather not be seen or they'd only stop her to question her.

The men hopped into the Jeep and pulled from the parking lot. She kept several blocks behind them. She plugged the dock location into her vehicle's GPS and waited for her system to provide her with the best route. Keeping far enough away from the Jeep to not be obvious but close enough to maintain sight of them, she headed in the same direction.

"YOU THINK SHE'LL follow us?" Merk asked Saul.

"Absolutely," Saul said. "She's determined to save her

friend."

"Admirable but foolish if she's not equipped to handle the danger she could be facing," Stone added.

"She's got guts. And she's loyal. As far as she's concerned, Daniel's responsible for her best friend's disappearance. No way in hell she'll let us get our hands on him and cut her out of this opportunity to find out more about Tammy."

"Guys," Dakota said, "this may be a decoy, a ruse, just like those emails sent to Tammy were supposedly from Daniel too."

The other men just nodded, all immersed in their own thoughts.

They reached a T-shaped intersection ten minutes later, deep into the docks, the water before them. Saul turned right, pulled alongside the far corner of one of the industrial-looking buildings and killed the Jeep's headlights. They all hopped out silently and set up to search the premises—one very large main building and several smaller buildings. A dark parking lot ran down the side of one of the buildings. It looked like an abandoned warehouse. And that was never good.

Merk and Stone took the front. Saul and Dakota slipped around the back, first checking out a small outbuilding the size of a garden shed. It was empty, the door hanging crookedly on its hinges. Next they approached the rear of the abandoned-looking warehouse with its first-floor windows mostly broken. They quietly pulled open the door, not surprised to find it unlocked.

No point in locking something when access could be gained via the busted-out windows.

They stepped inside and listened but found only silence.

They did a quick search of the ground floor. It was empty. They met their other two team members in the middle, splitting up again; each team of two went up one of the two staircases to check the second floor.

Despite the email, they had no guarantee Daniel had ever been in this building. Also no guarantee Daniel was still here or even if he had sent the cry for help.

Up here were rooms—probably used as offices at one time—on both sides of a hallway. Saul thought he heard something. With a finger to his lips, he slipped to the side along one wall. *Might have been a snuffle. Somebody sleeping? Maybe trying to sleep.* He peered into the darkness, waiting for his eyes to adjust. No windows were on this level, and the evening sun had gone down, leaving just a gloomy darkness. Not the pitch black of night, but more shadows than anything. He glanced into the first room, stepped quietly across the hallway to checked the opposite room. Nothing. He signaled to Dakota who went in the opposite direction.

Saul came up behind him, and they did a quick sweep of the third room, finding in its far back corner empty food wrappers. Fast food, chocolate bars. They frowned and found a pile of blankets in another corner. They continued to search the upstairs until a distinctive thud rippled through the building. Instantly they froze at the sound, waiting for another, then backtracked and headed toward the source.

Coming around a corner, weapons out, they approached the last hall to be checked upstairs. More empty offices, more footsteps in the dust and dirt. On high alert, they rounded one more corner, ready. And found Stone and Merk back to back, standing over a body on the floor, their weapons at the ready.

Merk gave a hand signal, pointing at Dakota to chase

after the killer. Dakota took off without making a sound.

Saul stepped closer and whispered, "Is it Daniel?"

Stone shook his head. "No." He used his cell phone's flashlight to spotlight the face of the body, the blood still pouring from his wound. "Looks to be a homeless man."

"Possibly, but that slice to his neck was made by a sharp knife," Merk noted.

"Do we think Daniel did this?" Saul asked.

Stone shook his head. "I'm not sure what's going on. I think somebody's after Daniel and found this man instead. This guy was in the wrong place at the wrong time and became collateral damage."

Merk's phone vibrated. After a listening only a few seconds, he said, "Come on back." Pocketing his phone, he told Stone and Saul, "He got away."

They did a quick search in the rest of the room but found no more fresh blood. Only one man had died here tonight, and it wasn't Daniel.

"Shit. Daniel's gone."

"Gone or never was here in the first place." The men looked at each other with grim faces. "What the hell is going on?"

Chapter 6

S HE PARKED BESIDE the Jeep and crept out of her car. Any other day, she'd be miles away from here, but, for a lead to save Tammy, she'd brave even this part of town. Thankfully the men were up ahead somewhere. She didn't know how helpful it would be if they saw her, as they would be quite pissed. But she couldn't afford to be left behind. Tammy was out there somewhere, just like Daniel was out there somewhere. And she was pretty damn sure, if she found one, she'd find the other. She crept into the building, her skin crawling with heightened sensations.

The dark shadows shifted with menace, echoing the emptiness that smelled of urine and spoke of danger. Shivering but determined, she took several cautious steps forward, searching the hallways and the rooms on the ground floor. All were completely empty. The men had to be here somewhere. Hearing footsteps, she hid behind a post. She wasn't sure if it was one of the guys or somebody else. Then she realized the footsteps were from a single person, creeping up the stairs. Shit. She bit her lip and made a quick decision.

The men were here, and, if they weren't on the main floor, they had to be upstairs with an intruder sneaking up on them. She hoped she hadn't signed her death warrant as she neared the stairwell and found it empty. Had she mistaken what she'd heard? Sticking to one side, she crept up the stairs, relieved when she heard Saul's voice. So the men were here. When Saul said, "Dead man," her heart froze.

She raced quietly in the direction of the voices, stopped at the doorway and studied the room. She could see the men standing around a crumpled figure on the floor. From the corner of her eye, she caught the whisper of a shadow and thought of the footsteps she thought she'd heard earlier. She backtracked to an earlier room and ducked inside.

She pulled out her phone and risked its backlight giving away her position by sending Saul a quick text. **You are not alone**. She gripped her cell phone to her shirt, hiding the backlight, which should turn off soon. Hopefully before the wrong guy saw it and found her. She didn't even have a weapon. How foolish of her.

She did a quick survey of her surroundings. Nothing was here, not even a stick. This place was full of dust and garbage. It looked like it had been abandoned years ago. She waited in the shadows, her breath raspy. Instinct told her to run downstairs to her car and to get the hell out of here before she got involved in something she couldn't get herself out of.

She backed up along the wall until she hit a corner and waited quietly. From her vantage point, she would hopefully see anybody who entered this room before they saw her. Maybe, if the intruder stepped in far enough, she could scoot out behind him and through the doorway, giving her a few seconds head start.

She jumped when her phone vibrated in her hand. She again risked her cell's backlight being seen by the bad guy to read the message. From Saul.

Stay hidden.

Really? You think I'm an idiot? Of course I'm staying hidden. Well, as best she could in an empty warehouse. She was tucked in a corner with walls on each side, her own phone lighting up to give away her position, but she had nowhere else to hide.

Then she heard footsteps running down the hallway, just on the other side of the same wall she was behind. And a kerfuffle ensued with raised voices, but they were now too far away for her to hear clearly. She gasped silently and sank to the floor. Next came the yelling.

"Rebel, are you there?"

She froze. That was Saul's voice. Or was it? What if it was someone else? Maybe it was a trick.

Then she heard Merk. "Rebel, it's okay. They are gone. Where are you?"

Then things got quiet. Too quiet.

She could hear heavy breathing nearby where she hadn't seen anyone earlier. Was the intruder in the room with her? Was he just outside in the hallway, leaning against the same wall she leaned against? Someone else was in this building. She froze, tried to still the panic within.

From her current position, she could hear the breathing—breathing where there shouldn't have been any. Breathing that said somebody else lay here in wait.

"She has to be here."

"Unless she's still hiding."

"Or she took off?"

"Where? Back to her car."

She closed her eyes, sending Saul a mental cry for help.

"Shh."

Silence descended.

Even the breathing near her had stopped.

She hugged her chest to her knees, while she held her breath and waited as footsteps approached. The sound of one person. Closer and closer and closer. She wanted to cry out. She shoved her hand over her mouth to still the screams threatening to erupt. She closed her eyes and listened to distant racing footsteps and the shouts of men as everyone took chase on the opposite end of this floor. So when a light shone on her face, she screamed.

"It's okay. It's me," Saul said. "It's okay."

She stared up at him, frozen. He reached out his arms and hauled her to her feet, wrapping her tight against his chest. Just that solid security of knowing he was here, that she wasn't alone, that the heavy breather wouldn't find her unprotected and vulnerable and open to attack, had her wrapping her arms around him and squeezing him tight. It took a few minutes of his hands gently stroking up and down her back for her to realize how badly she was shaking. He murmured gentle words against her ear. Words she barely understood. She focused on that.

"It's okay. Calm down, Rebel. It's all right."

Finally she tilted her head back and took a deep breath. "Did you find him?"

"Find who?"

She pointed to the doorway. "A man outside that door. I could hear him breathing. Just a heavy, rasping, guttural tone that terrified me."

He bolted out the door. She could hear his footsteps. She winced, hating to be left alone again, but he returned almost as fast. "Whoever it was is gone now." He paused. "And that's why you didn't call out when we yelled for you?"

She stared at him, her gaze still wide with fright. "I didn't dare give away my position. He was closer than you were."

Saul nodded. "I wondered." He gave her a gentle shake. "What are you doing here? Why didn't you stay away?"

"Even though I'm terrified of this place, I wanted to be here. If I can find out anything that will help me save my friend, I'm doing it," she said with a hard determination. "I don't care if it's stupid or if it's dangerous."

He groaned. "I know it's hard, honey. I know that. But you are not helping Tammy by getting hurt yourself. Or by distracting us from a murderer and now this other guy."

She brushed loose strands of hair off her forehead. "I know that. Really I do, but what am I supposed to do? I'd do anything to save her."

He turned and wrapped an arm around her shoulders and led her from the room. "Is this where you thought you saw someone standing?" He pointed to the wall just outside the room she'd been in.

Rebel nodded. "Yes."

He turned his flashlight to study the spot. Outside of misshapen footprints in the dust, there was nothing.

"Any idea who it was?" she asked.

"No. We found a dead man, homeless from the looks of it. Only he's not been dead long."

"You're sure it's not Daniel?"

He glanced at her. "It's not Daniel, and I doubt Daniel killed him."

She shrugged. "How can you be so sure?"

"Because we know his brother. Daniel could be a loser in life and someone who we would like to see buck up, take responsibility and be a better man, but that doesn't mean he's a complete write-off. Whenever there's an opportunity, we give people that chance."

HER DEDICATION TO finding her friend was admirable. But, Christ, he'd almost had a heart attack when he'd seen her crouched in the corner. But he knew there was no talking to her. Loyalty was something he could understand. Even hard-headed bullheadedness. It was impossible to talk her out of these attitudes which he could fully relate to. He knew she was determined to follow them. But, when he had seen the docks' surroundings, the abandoned buildings and the overall decrepit state of the area, he'd hoped she had turned around. Or at least stayed in her car. But, of course, she hadn't. When they'd found the dead man, Dakota had taken off in the direction of his murderer, but obviously more than one intruder had been here.

It chilled him inside to think she had heard a man's breathing, heavy and harsh enough to be positioned very near her, like on the opposite side of one interior wall. Not much structurally between them. He didn't know if she had any self-defense training to handle herself in a situation like this, but nobody ever had enough skills. Being here was asking for trouble. He was just grateful he'd found her before anything else bad happened.

He nudged her toward where he'd left Stone. Although Saul didn't think anybody was still around, he couldn't leave the homeless man here; yet Saul didn't want her to see the dead body either. "Let's join the others. It'll be chaos soon. The cops are on the way."

She glanced at him. "Will they care enough to find out who died? Who did this to him?"

He nodded. "Yes, they will. With the slit throat this guy has, it was a little too professional."

"So it's more about the killer of the victim?" she asked incredulously.

He frowned at her. "That's not what I meant. Don't twist my words around."

She snapped, "Why? I haven't seen the cops exactly jumping on Tammy's case."

"You don't know they haven't done anything either. The problem is, she's disappeared, and they can only follow so many leads before they hit a dead end. When they do, what do you expect them to do next? They can't just pull her out of thin air. If she has willfully disappeared, she's done a hell of a good job of it. If she's been kidnapped or killed, and no signs were left behind, it's very hard to investigate further when they've exhausted what leads they do have. Sometimes you have to sit and wait."

"I know that," she said. "I'm just so frustrated because I can't find anything."

"And the police have a lot more resources available. They haven't forgotten her. Plus finding out more about this man and his murderer are as important to giving the dead man's family closure as it could be to finding Daniel and Tammy."

She shrugged off his hand and distanced herself by moving away another step.

He turned to see Merk, Stone and Dakota walking toward them. "Did you get them?"

"No," Stone snapped, obviously aggravated.

"Both of them escaped?" Rebel asked, her voice incredulous. "From the four of you?"

The men turned their gazes on her, anger and frustration clearly etched on their faces. Saul reached out and squeezed her arm. "Yes, both. It's dark. This is their space. They would have bolt-holes that we don't know about."

She sighed. "Look, I'm sorry. I'm not accusing you of not being good enough or anything. I was just so hoping we would find something useful here."

"And maybe we will. Have patience." Saul turned to the others. "I guess there is no power in this place, is there?"

"Even if the power was still connected, no working lightbulb has been left here," Dakota said from his side. "Cops are about ten minutes out. I already called this in to Ice."

"Right, she'll connect this case to Tammy's and Daniel's cases."

"Well, that's something," Rebel said. "Maybe if they bring in forensics, they could find something." She turned to study the building and then shrugged. "Although how they could possibly find anything of value here, I don't know."

"And that's the problem. No police department has the resources to fingerprint a massive place like this or to check for DNA among all this trash. This place is a squatter's paradise and a veritable hygienic nightmare. It's been used by the homeless for decades probably."

Merk shone his cell phone light on the victim and said, "Anybody run his ID?"

Dakota spoke up. "I did. There's nothing on him."

"Did you check his shoes?" Rebel asked.

The men turned to look at her.

She shrugged. "I've heard stories of some homeless people keeping their valuables in their shoes. Everybody steals from these homeless people's pockets and backpacks, their carts and their bags, but nobody steals a homeless man's ratty shoes. The only time the shoes on a homeless person are removed is when they're dead."

Dakota stepped forward and said, "I didn't check. But I will now." He pulled a pair of gloves from his pocket, slipped them on and pulled the shoes off the man's feet. Underneath the sole of one was a twenty-dollar bill. "Interesting."

"A twenty is a lot of money for this man."

The other shoe held a locket.

Rebel rushed forward. "Let me see that," she snapped.

Dakota laid it in his gloved hands. "Don't touch it, just in case."

She shook her head. "There won't be any fingerprints left on that," she said. "I need to open it. It looks very much like Tammy's."

Having difficulty with the tiny mechanism, finally Dakota managed to open the locket. Inside lay a picture of a woman and a child. "It's Tammy's." Rebel stared down at the dead man. "Where did he find Tammy's locket?"

"That could explain why he's dead," Saul said in a determined voice. "Come here away from the body please."

She turned to look at him. "Are you squeamish?"

"No, I'm not. But I do like to honor the dead."

She cringed. "Again I'm sorry. I just get so focused on one thing, and I tend to forget all the niceties that go with it."

"As much as we admire your determination to help your friend, you can't impede the police investigation. Somebody killed this man, and he deserves justice as much as the person who may have hurt Tammy."

She nodded and stepped back. "Still this is a clue. Somehow in this man's travels, which I can't imagine were very far, he came across Tammy's locket. That it's in his shoe means either it was worth keeping or he wanted to hide it." She turned to Dakota. "Was anything in his pockets?"

He shook his head. "They'd been cleaned out."

She nodded. "Chances are somebody was looking for the locket."

"That's an assumption we can't afford to make," Merk warned. "We follow evidence. We find clues. Assumptions are good in terms of discussing hypotheses and options. However, we can't count on them yet."

She groaned and stared at the dark ceiling. "I understand that. I just need to find Tammy."

Saul looked at her. "We understand when a friend goes missing. That's why we're here." He studied her for a long moment. "Is there another reason as well?"

"No. She's just a very good friend of mine."

Then they heard the sirens. Dakota said, "I'll direct them up."

As soon as he disappeared, Rebel said, "I'll go downstairs and wait."

"Wait for what?" Merk asked.

She shot him a look. "Wait for whatever you guys do next."

"Meaning, if we don't include you, you'll follow us?" Stone asked.

Stone was such a big man but such a gentle giant. Rebel took no offense. "Yes, I will. If you lead me to Daniel, Daniel leads me to Tammy." She spun on her heels downstairs in the dark.

Saul glanced at the others, his gaze questioning. They looked at each other and then nodded. "Okay," Saul said, "I'll stay with her. Let me know how this goes."

Chapter 7

REBEL DIDN'T KNOW what to do. How Tammy's locket was in this vagrant's shoe was a mystery she couldn't deal with right now. She'd been shocked at the poor man's fate, but to see that locket so out of place was so very wrong; she just had to get out of there.

She bolted down the dark stairs, knowing she was going at a speed that would guarantee a broken ankle if she stepped wrong. But she couldn't hold herself back; she couldn't stop herself from escaping here. She didn't dare drive away because she needed the police to understand just how important this clue was. Tammy *always* wore that locket. She loved it. It was a connection to her mother, and her mother always wore a matching one.

All Rebel could think about was the fact that Tammy might be dead. She'd never willingly give up that necklace. And if the locket had been taken from her … Rebel just couldn't let her mind keep going in that direction.

Once outside her wild flight slowed. The police were everywhere. One of the cops motioned to her. She gazed at him, not sure she could talk to him yet.

Suddenly a strong arm reached across her shoulders. She didn't even jerk in surprise. She knew Saul's touch. He led her to the police and introduced them both. She stayed silent, not knowing how to come down from this shock.

"The locket," the policeman asked, "are you sure it's from your friend Tammy?"

She nodded numbly. "She always wore it," she whispered. "It was very precious to her."

The policeman nodded. "We'll take a statement from both of you. Can you come down to the station tomorrow morning?"

She shuddered and then nodded. "I can."

"That sounds best for us as well," Saul said. "The other men are upstairs with the body."

The officer looked at her and said, "I'll need your contact information and address. And please stay in town while we get to the bottom of this."

She wrapped her arms around her chest and said, "I'm not going anywhere until I know where my friend is." She gave him the information he'd asked for, thankful she didn't have to stick around here for too much longer.

When she could, she walked over to her car, unlocked it and sat down in the driver's seat. When the passenger side opened and Saul slid in beside her, she wasn't surprised either. She locked her gaze on the building before her.

Despite her mad rush to escape that place, it was the one connection she had to Tammy, and it was so damn hard to leave it now. She also knew she couldn't do anything else here. The police would check the entire building top to bottom. She already saw them setting up generators outside to give them the power needed to run the portable lights being carted inside. She could only hope Tammy's body wasn't lying discarded in a corner, unloved and forgotten by the world. A sob caught in the back of her throat. She placed her hand over her mouth and closed her eyes. She was close to the breaking point; she just didn't dare do it now. She couldn't drive under those conditions, and she didn't want Saul to see her in that state regardless.

"What will you do now?" she asked.

"We'll return to our temporary lodgings for the night," he said quietly. "We'll pick this up again in the morning."

She shook her head. "You've only been here for part of a day. Look how much you've already shaken out of the woodwork." She turned to look at him. "I've been trying since forever to find any information and got nowhere."

"Sometimes it works out that way," he said.

She stared at him wordlessly and then felt the resurgence of tears in the back of her eyes. "She's dead, isn't she?"

He reached over, grabbed her by the shoulders and gave her a gentle shake. "No. You can't think that way."

He tugged her into his arms and just held her. It seemed so long since anybody had been there for her that she wondered if it was okay to lean on him, even just for the moment. With everything else going on, myriad emotions boiled through her, overwhelming her. She burst into tears.

He never said a word; he just held her close.

When her emotional storm spent itself, she lifted her head, which had been tucked up against his shoulder, and stared out at the darkness. "I can't stand to think she's lying lost and broken somewhere, that somebody could have done something to her. She was so very special."

He reached up gently and wiped the tears off her cheeks. "Don't speak of her in the past tense. We have to keep up the hope that she's alive."

She nodded, settled back on her side of the car and wiped her tears. "I should go home and get some rest."

"Yes, you should. It's probably been days since you've had a good night's sleep."

"I haven't slept." She laughed. "How could I?"

"And again you're no good to her if you can't look after yourself." He studied her face. "Let me drive you home. You're in no shape to drive yourself."

She stared down at her hands, still trembling in shock. She took a deep breath and told herself to smarten up. But her pep talk failed miserably.

A knock on the window on Saul's side startled her. He rolled down the window, and Stone leaned in and said, "We're ready to go to Richard's."

Saul nodded. "I'll take her home. You want to follow and pick me up?" He motioned toward Rebel. "She's in no shape to drive right now."

Stone studied her face and then nodded. "We'll follow you there." He tapped the top of the car and walked over to Saul's Jeep with the keys in his hand.

Saul looked at her. "Okay?"

She nodded. She handed him the keys, and the two of them changed places. She watched as he started up her old car and reversed out of the alleyway. He handled the car with a competence she expected. With that, she settled back and let somebody else take care of her for once.

HE COULDN'T IMAGINE she accepted help very often. Whether she knew it or not, she kept walls up and that worked most of the time. But she'd hit a personal limit. He'd seen it happen time and time again. Not only had she been fighting to find her friend but dead bodies were unsettling. Finding that locket was a huge step forward, but it was also a serious step backward in terms of understanding where her friend was. It did not mean she was dead, but, after ten days, with something like that showing up, it, … well, … was not a good sign.

Saul hadn't wanted to leave the crime scene. He could only hope the police shared the information they found. He planned to go back in the daylight and see if he could find any evidence that Tammy had been in that building.

Plus he also would check out where the homeless man was known to hang out. Just because he was in the building at the end of his life did not mean Tammy had been there too. She could've been anywhere along his route. He could've taken the locket off her dead body for that matter. Or he could've seen it on the ground someplace where she might've been involved in a struggle. There were endless possibilities.

He drove to Rebel's apartment. He knew the area well. He had friends living not too far from here. When he drove up in front of a large brick apartment building, he nudged her. "Is this your place?"

Startled, she looked at him, a dazed look in her eyes. "How did you know where I lived?"

"I heard you tell the policeman."

She had a right to be suspicious. He just didn't want her suspicious of *him*. She contemplated his answer; then she reached up and rubbed her face. "I'm sorry. I'm just not myself right now."

He parked the vehicle, got out and walked around to her side of the car. She still sat in the passenger seat, staring at the building. She needed time to work through this. He opened her door and helped her to her feet. "Come on. Let's get you inside."

The Jeep pulled up behind him. Saul and Rebel walked up to the entranceway, and she punched in a security code into the keypad on the wall. The door unlocked in front of them. He pulled it open and held it for her to walk through. The other three men waited in the Jeep, watching. He gave them a half wave, walked her inside and to the elevator. He studied her carefully. He wasn't sure she should be alone right now. "You have anybody you can call? Any other friends or family who could stay with you?"

She shook her head. "Only Tammy. I would call Tammy."

Damn. That just triggered another memory of Tammy. Not that Rebel was likely to stop thinking about her best friend under these circumstances.

On the third floor the elevator door opened. He gently grasped her arm above the elbow, nudging her into the hallway. With the keys from her vehicle in his hand, he checked for an apartment key. Sure enough, he tried the door, and the selected key worked. He opened the door and led her inside.

And she froze. "What happened?"

His gaze sharpened. He kicked the door shut and put Rebel between him and the door. He pulled out his weapon with one hand and his phone with other, saying, "Get up here."

He put away his phone and left her backed against the front door to search her destroyed apartment. He could see most of it from this vantage point but not enough to ease his concerns. Still, he had to leave her to do a full sweep. Her kitchen table and the kitchen drawers were tossed to the ground. The living room couch cushions had been slashed open. He noted all this while running a timeline through his head. Had Tammy been kidnapped? Had she told them about Rebel? Or had whoever killed or kidnapped Tammy known that she and Rebel were best friends? Did Daniel tell the kidnappers that? Or did the kidnappers/murderers find Rebel lurking around Daniel's apartment building too, just like Saul and his team did? That alone revealed Rebel had some deep connection to Daniel and/or Tammy. Were the women best friends enough that Rebel would hold something for Tammy?

He hadn't even thought to question Rebel on that last aspect. But, with Tammy and Daniel both being in IT, espionage was not an unlikely leap. The fact that Daniel was suspected of hacking into his employer's system and creating coding errors somehow played together. Saul didn't understand how yet, but he would.

He made a quick sweep of the tiny one-bedroom apartment. By the time he made it back to Rebel—still leaning against the door, her face stricken—a knock at the door made Rebel jump. Saul checked the peephole and then let his friends in.

They stepped inside, took one look and Stone let out a low whistle. "Well, this is an interesting development."

Something about his tone of voice and wording caught Rebel's attention. She turned on him. "Interesting? This is *interesting* for you? This is destructive. This is horrific. This is my entire life here."

Stone looked at her pointedly. "And yet, you're alive. So they knew you weren't here. They went through your property, went through all your possessions. What were they looking for?"

Saul watched her face go blank.

Then her jaw dropped. "You think they were looking for something?" She shook her head in bewilderment. "Looking for what?" she cried out. "I don't have anything. Hell,

Tammy made way more money than I did. Why would they not destroy her place instead?" She stared at the men, her gaze going from one to the other and then back again. "Why me?"

Dakota stepped in. "That's what we'll find out. One of the first questions we need to know is did Tammy, at any time in the last few months, give you anything to safeguard for her?"

That was the very question Saul wanted answered; he stepped closer and peered at Rebel's face, looking for any sign of subterfuge.

She stared at the men and shrugged her shoulders. "No, of course not. Why would she?"

"She could have found something damning at work, and she needed you to hold on to it, on the off chance something happened to her."

She frowned, her focus remaining on the men. "She didn't give me anything to hold or keep. I didn't know of anything potentially dangerous in her world. She would've told me."

"Did she feel the same way about you as you feel about her?" Saul asked quietly.

She turned her gaze to his. "Yes. We've been best friends since forever."

"Maybe she wouldn't tell you about this, seeing it would bring danger to your doorstep."

He watched the wheels in her mind turn, and then a stricken look took over her face as she realized something. "That's exactly what Tammy would do," she whispered. "As I would for her."

"And that's why this is interesting," Stone said. "Because this changes our avenues of thinking completely. Whoever came here was looking for something, for whatever reason, whether she told them or they assumed so because of your close association."

"Or because Daniel told them," she said bitterly. "He was always a troublemaker."

Chapter 8

S HE STARED AT her destroyed belongings, rubbing her temple out of habit. Nothing made sense in her world anymore. Only a single kitchen chair still sat upright on four legs. She picked it up from the pile of garbage underneath it and repositioned it to a more stable spot and collapsed on it. "I slept here last night."

Saul didn't even want to acknowledge his thoughts that immediately followed that statement.

"Why? Why do this?" It was a stupid question because she knew the answer, but she couldn't stop herself from asking the obvious. "None of this makes any sense."

"It made sense to the person who did it," Saul said. "We may not know the logic behind this yet, but there will be some. It may not even make sense to us when we do know. But the person who did this had a reason, and they took a lot of time trashing your apartment. So who would know you weren't here today?"

She stared at him. "I have no idea. Anybody could have seen me leave, but how would they know how long I would be gone?"

"Unless they saw you at Daniel's apartment building. And maybe had seen you at Daniel's building a lot this last week."

"But then they would've seen me with you guys."

Saul's voice, low and hard, said, "And maybe they didn't care if you did come back. Maybe they were hoping you were here so they could ask you themselves about what they were looking for." He didn't want to scare her needlessly, but she could no longer ignore the fact that she was a target now. By the expression of horror on her face, she understood fully.

The other men contemplated that concept in silence. One by one they nodded.

"Given the fact we have two people missing and one dead body, chances are very good that's exactly what would've happened here," Stone said. "In which case, it's a damn good thing you weren't present."

Her heart beat wildly, and her accelerated pulse rate throbbed in her head. She took one long slow inhale, then another, all while staring at the floor. *Focus on that*, she told herself. *I have some control over this mess before me, if only to clean it up.* All her kitchen cupboards had been busted and their contents dumped on the ground. The drawers had been opened and dropped. Even the contents of her fridge were shattered on the floor. Broken glass and ruined food was everywhere.

"You have insurance?" Merk asked.

"I have renter's insurance but have no idea if it covers this type of an issue."

Saul's phone rang. He pulled it from his pocket. "Hello, Detective Wilson. What did you find?" He listened for a long moment and then said, "Okay, we've had a development here. Rebel's apartment has been vandalized. A thorough job, not just some punk kids. The contents of the fridge dumped, couch cushions sliced open, things like that."

She watched as he nodded at something the detective said, then turned to look to the front door.

"No, it doesn't appear to be a forced entry."

Her mind blanked at that. How could they not have forced their way in? If they hadn't, that would mean they had a way in of their own, and her heart sank.

Because Tammy had a spare key to her apartment.

Jesus, when would this nightmare end? It would take days to clean up this mess. She couldn't imagine the cost of everything she'd just lost in terms of monetary value. Sure, she had insurance, but would it cover this? She had no idea as she'd never made a claim. What she did know was she had no wish to even begin to sort through what was usable and what wasn't. Broken dishes were mixed with food among the other debris. Was anything here worth keeping? Did she care?

Hysterical laughter rose at the back of her throat. With her gut clenched, she clamped down on it hard. She wanted to be any place but here right now. And yet, she had no place else to go.

Saul stepped forward, sliding his phone back into his pocket. "They found no sign of Tammy in the building where we found the homeless man."

She blinked up at him. Relief washed through her. "So she still could be alive?"

"It's possible. It's not very likely, but we can't give up hope."

She nodded and looked around. "There has to be a reason why they came here, and the only connection is Tammy."

"And," Dakota said quietly, "if Tammy was caught up in something unintentionally, you're getting dragged into it yourself. Their trail has now led to you. If they were looking for something and didn't find it this time, I can guarantee you that, if they think you have anything to do with that, you could be snatched next."

She pulled her legs up, her heels on the edge of the chair and her knees tight to her chest as she rewrapped her arms around them. "How do I find Tammy if these guys are after me?"

"You keep yourself safe while you let a lot of other people look for Tammy."

She shook her head. "That's not good enough. A lot of people were supposedly looking for her last week, and nobody gave a damn."

"And maybe this is all happening because somebody realized you wouldn't let this go," Merk said. "Maybe they are scaring you off. Maybe they are chasing you away, leaving them free and clear. What I do know is, if you cross the line any further and really piss them off, you won't survive either."

She stared at him dully. "How am I supposed to walk away from a friend who's in need?"

Her words seemed to have struck a chord. All the men fell silent.

Merk shook his head. "We can't tell you to do that because we're the same. Friendships and loyalty, they matter in our world."

"And Tammy matters in my world." She stared at the remnants of her apartment. She waved her hand around at the destruction and said, "That means I'm not safe here anymore either."

"Time to pack a bag," Saul said.

"First," Stone said, "can you tell us how somebody might've gotten into your apartment?"

"That's easy. Tammy had a key."

She walked into her bedroom, and, even though she was prepared for what she'd find, the destruction still brought tears to her eyes. She slapped a hand over her mouth to hold back her instinctual cry. Her beautiful duvets and pillows were slashed and pulled apart. Feathers were everywhere. The place had been annihilated—her night table, her dresser drawers, everything tossed.

She turned back to the men, tears in her eyes. "Are you sure they were looking for something? Because this looks like wanton destruction. Not a methodical search."

"They'd have searched first and then left it like this, destroyed, for the police to find."

She nodded. "Bastards."

Stepping into a clear spot in the bedroom, she faced her tossed closet. She pulled out her large travel bag, set it on the bed and sorted through the piles of clothing on the floor but was hard-pressed to find anything usable. Everything she picked up had been sliced. Multiple times. She didn't need to be a shrink to note this was done in extreme anger.

In the back of her bag, she found her waterproof see-through ziplock folder where she kept her passport and important personal papers. It was intact. She grabbed it and stuffed it in her purse and walked into the bathroom to get a few toiletries. She wasn't much of a shopper, so she didn't buy a whole lot in terms of material things. She didn't like knickknacks. She preferred good paintings and lots of white space on her walls …

The trouble was, she needed enough possessions to survive. And she barely had that right now. Back in the closet she dug through the piles and pulled out a heavy sweater, her coat and several pairs of shoes. She didn't need them now but if they'd survived she could use them in a few months.

Oddly enough they hadn't destroyed all the things in her closet, although all of it had been thrown to the floor. She guessed that the slashing of the topmost layer of her clothes was for added emphasis.

Saul stood in the doorway. "Can you see if they've added anything to this room?"

She spun, startled. "What you mean by added?"

"Planted evidence that would indicate you had something to do with Tammy's disappearance."

"How could you even contemplate that?" she cried out in horror.

He shrugged. "We've encountered a lot of assholes in this world. The things they do don't always make sense to us, but it can cause a lot of pain for others. We also need to know when you were here last. What was their window of opportunity?"

"I slept here last night," she said, pointing and staring forlornly at her destroyed bed. "I got up around 8:00 a.m., and I think I was out the door by ten."

"You don't have any security cameras here, do you?"

She shook her head. "But lots of security cameras are up and down the hallway."

"We will check those."

"They will be busted. This wasn't vandalism. This was rage acted out, and they had fun doing this." She held up a bra that had been cut in two. "This is not normal behavior."

"There's nothing normal about any of this," he assured her. "I'm glad you're able to pack something in your bag. When you're done, bring it to the front hall." And he disappeared from the doorway.

She stared at the spot and cried out, "Why? I don't have any place to go."

"Well," Saul said, appearing once more, "you aren't staying here tonight." Once again he disappeared around the corner.

She could go to a hotel for the night but for how long? That was an expense she couldn't justify right now.

Not even after taking a week off from work as "vacation" time to look for Tammy.

Instead of finding her, Rebel had been caught up in the same chaos with no end in sight.

BACK IN THE kitchen Saul motioned toward the bedroom and said, "She's packing a bag."

The others nodded.

"Does she have anywhere to go?" Stone asked. "And the cameras in the hallway are broken. She needs to make sure she has somewhere safe."

Saul shrugged. "She says Tammy's is where she would've gone for help, but, without her, Rebel doesn't have anywhere else to turn."

The men winced. "That's got to be hard," Dakota said. "You know? Thinking about this from a different angle, these people all have one thing in common."

"What people?" Merk asked. He leaned against the fridge, his arms crossed over his chest. "And how does it relate to this mess?"

"All of them work for the same company."

The men stared at him in consideration.

Dakota continued, "Two were in IT. One was known to play games for whatever reason. We're talking programmers here. We're talking people who can cause serious damage or be coerced into causing serious damage. Also people who can steal information, money, damn near anything through their own computer skills."

"You think Tammy and Daniel might've been involved in something like that?" Merk asked.

Dakota shrugged. "One of them, yes. Probably dragged the other one in, either deliberately or accidentally."

"And Rebel?" Saul asked. "You're thinking that, because people know she's good friends with Tammy, they'd assume she might be holding something for her friend?"

"Or somebody in the company has been pulling strings," Stone said, "or making it look like Daniel's been pulling strings and has now decided that, if Rebel won't let Tammy go, then Rebel's become a liability."

"But then why destroy her property? Why not just kill her?" Merk asked.

At the gasp in the hallway, the men turned to see Rebel standing there, her face pale, a large bag at her feet.

Dakota carried on, his gaze steady. "Because the bad guys could always use the two women's close friendship against each other. Threaten to hurt Tammy if Rebel didn't cooperate and vice versa. There's always the chance that Tammy didn't give Rebel anything. Or that Rebel knows more than she thinks she knows."

"But I don't know anything," Rebel cried out.

"Tell us about the work environment at your job," Stone said, directing her focus there.

"The telecommunication company is huge." She named a couple bigwig corporate types at her location here in San Diego.

Saul nodded. "And you're in marketing?"

"Yes. All I do is graphics and ad copy."

"How much do you know about the IT work that

Tammy and Daniel did?" Merk asked.

"Tammy rarely spoke about it. She said security was a big component in her job, both within the software itself and how few personnel were entrusted with any knowledge of it."

"And Daniel?" Stone asked.

"He was a bit of a bragger, but he never really gave any details, just that what he was doing was super important and made him a big cheese. Honestly I hardly listened. The man was insufferable."

"What's the chance somebody else in the company pulled all those tricks and blamed Daniel?" Merk asked. "And when Daniel became a liability, they took care of him and possibly Tammy at the same time."

She frowned. "You think somebody else in the company is doing this? Why? Who?"

"Can you think of anybody else who might have a connection to the three of you?" Stone asked, prodding her.

She stared at him and then slowly shook her head. "No one other than those we work with."

"And Tammy was in a relationship with Daniel, and that makes you connected to him too," Saul added.

"Of course, but only because I was Tammy's best friend. I was talking her out of resuming any relationship with Daniel. I even brought it up at work, but I was discreet about it. Still, I imagine we could have easily been overheard within the marketing cubicles or in the breakroom or if I crossed paths with Tammy in the copier room or in the elevator. But I just can't imagine what issue would necessitate killing people though."

"That's already been brought up," Saul said. "Once you start talking about programming and telecommunications, we could be looking at espionage or even terrorism."

"Good luck with getting information from the company."

"Why is that?" Stone asked. "So far a lot of them have been forthcoming and cooperative. At least the half we spoke to. Our boss called the others and questioned them but I haven't heard anyone being difficult."

She shrugged. "Yet I'm sure they were very closed-mouthed and secretive when it comes to security details."

"How many people are in the IT department?" Saul asked with a frown.

She focused on Saul and frowned, concentrating. "I think eight, including the supervisor."

"You know who the supervisor is?" Merk asked.

"Samantha Clapton is the supervisor now. She replaced Gordon. He was a nice guy. He was there for twenty years. Then one day he just didn't come to work. According to Daniel, he got in an argument with the upper-level guys, quit and walked out."

The men stared at her, Merk already on his phone, texting someone.

She shrugged, didn't understand their reaction. "I don't know if it's true or not. I only know what Tammy told me. She was concerned because Gordon was a good guy and had been a huge help to her when she first started at the company. She hated to think he'd been shafted in some way."

The men nodded.

"Any idea what his last name is?" Merk asked.

She shook her head. "They took his name off the company's website. I certainly don't know what went on. Some employees made various comments, gossiping that he done something wrong, but Tammy was adamant he hadn't done anything wrong. Gordon didn't like Samantha. They'd been going toe to toe over some of the security measures in the company."

"How long ago did he leave?" Dakota asked.

She pursed her lips. "A couple months ago. Daniel was promoted soon afterward. He retired. There wasn't anything suspicious about his exit."

"And when did all the problems with Daniel start?" Saul asked.

Her head bounced back and forth like a four-way tennis match, the guys peppering her with one question after another. "A long time ago. Then he appeared to clean up his act."

"How long ago exactly?" Merk asked.

She shrugged. "Tammy would know. They should have promoted Tammy anyway. She was the kind not to take bullshit from staff or management. Daniel, on the other hand, could be easily manipulated by a great pair of legs and boobs."

Chapter 9

A T THE ODD silence, she glared at the men. "That was not Tammy. Even though Tammy is beautiful, slim, would easily have been the most popular girl at school. And she was the most popular girl at work. Still she didn't have to pull any kind of stunts to get her promotions."

"Maybe if she had, she would have gotten the promotion over Daniel," Merk said.

She studied Merk's face, seeing an understanding of how life worked and often didn't work. "Yes, quite possibly. But she and Gordon got along very well without any of that."

"And the new supervisor?" Stone asked.

"Well, Tammy just wasn't into that kind of a thing."

"What kind of thing?" Dakota asked.

"You know, when you're at a job, and there's a clique, a group of the in-crowd, where they all fawn over the one in power just like high school all over again? The department slowly diverged into that. Daniel was on the inside."

"Tammy was on the outside, I presume." At Rebel's nod, Saul asked, "And who else was on the inside?"

"A couple others. Both men."

"Of course, since the new supervisor is a woman, Samantha."

She shot Saul a bright smile. "You got it."

Saul exchanged glances with Dakota. "Sounds like we

need to talk to Samantha."

"Good luck with that," Rebel said. "She's perpetually unavailable. Unless you're law enforcement, she won't say anything to you." She pulled out her phone and hit the proper contact name. "I'll call her right now."

They all waited as the phone rang and rang then went to voicemail." She didn't bother leaving a message. Pocketing her phone, Rebel said, "Like I said, she's hard to talk to. She'd have seen my number and said, hell no!"

The men nodded. "We'll get her to talk. But first things first. Where will you stay for the night? And you should call the insurance company in the morning to deal with this."

She grimaced. "I'll sleep in my car downstairs in the secured parking lot. Then start fresh in the morning." She watched Saul's mouth open and shook her head. "I'm fine in the car. It'll be safe and secure down there. It will allow me to get a few hours of sleep and recover from the shock," Rebel said, hopefully in a pragmatic, reasonable tone of voice. "In the morning, I'll start cleaning up this mess."

Saul shook his head. "Look around you, Rebel. You can't stay here, and you can't stay in your car *anywhere*."

Rebel, not liking what he had to say, glared at him and snapped, "Why not?"

"Because whoever was here might still be keeping an eye on the place and will know you came back. They have already checked out your vehicle and will be watching it too."

"That's a big assumption," she protested.

"We have to assume that," Saul said, his tone steady. "And, if you weren't dealing with so many hits one after another, you would see that. Right now you aren't thinking straight. It's up to us to make sure you don't get hurt or any deeper into trouble."

She narrowed her gaze at him. "Are you saying I got myself into trouble thus far?"

He glared at her. "Don't twist my words around," he snapped. "You're not staying in your car overnight. That's final."

"Where do you suggest I stay? Should I go to Tammy's place? But, if they trashed my place, then they should have trashed hers."

"Tammy's apartment is a possibility but not alone." Saul frowned. "Actually that's not a bad idea." He glanced at the guys, all silently agreeing with him. "We never did get much time to search her place."

"Search for what?"

He shrugged. "Who knows?"

"Well, I know her very well. There was nothing hidden about Tammy. She was very open. Very stable, nonconfrontational. She'd never do anything dangerous."

"And yet, she's in trouble," Merk said. "So you're a little more confrontational, a little more living on the edge. What's next for you?"

She glared at him.

"Note the evidence," Merk said in exasperation. "Look around you. This is hardly something we've made up."

She raised her hands in frustration. "What am I supposed to do then?"

Stone stepped forward. "Go to a hotel for the night. One you've never been to before. Give a fake name. Pay cash for the room, for anything related to your stay," Stone said. "If you don't have enough cash on you, do not go to an ATM. We'll give you enough cash to cover tonight's lodgings. From the safety of your hotel room, using the hotel phone, contact your insurance company. In the meantime, get ready to speak to the police once more. They should be here anytime now."

"Like they'll care."

"Yes, they will," Saul said. "It's all related to Tammy's disappearance, now Daniel's, plus we have the murderer of the homeless man involved too. I believe this has all just escalated in the police's eyes."

"How wrong is it that Tammy's disappearance alone didn't take priority?"

Saul glared at her. "It's not like Tammy is the only case the whole police department is working right now. Stop being difficult. Just because they couldn't find her right away doesn't mean they weren't trying to all this time."

She groaned. "I understand that in theory, but it's so damn frustrating. I just want her home safe and sound."

"And we don't want you to come face-to-face with the men who did this to your apartment or who killed an unarmed homeless man," Stone said, his voice solid, unmovable. "So, until we resolve this, you shouldn't be alone."

"Even if I go to a hotel, I'll be alone."

Just then a knock came at the door. Saul opened it to admit the police. The detective assigned to Tammy's case stepped in. He looked at Rebel. "Glad to see you're still okay."

She nodded. She didn't know what to say to him anymore. Still she couldn't stop asking the same question, "Anything new on Tammy?"

He shook his head. "It was her locket that you found at the warehouse. It had smudges of fingerprints but none clear enough to get anything from, so we don't have any further leads."

"Is anybody tracking the homeless man's area to see if maybe he happened upon Tammy's body?" Rebel asked, choking up a bit on that last word.

"We have cops out canvassing the area. But it will be hard to see anything until daylight."

"True enough." Rebel shook her head. Time was against her and Tammy, who would go through another night in whatever situation she was in. It so wasn't fair. "It should've been me," she said suddenly.

"What should have been you?" the detective asked.

"I should've picked her up. I should've insisted. Then she wouldn't have been traveling alone on the bus that night."

"That doesn't mean it should've been you," Saul said quietly. "It means, maybe it would've warded this off temporarily, or maybe both of you would've been taken that night."

She shot him a look. "I just can't help wishing I'd done more."

"And that's a sentiment every family member and friend of a deceased or missing person feels," the detective said. "We're doing everything we can. This appears to be connected to Daniel's disappearance and now to potentially our latest victim. But don't think we've forgotten about Tammy's disappearance, because we haven't."

She turned her gaze away. She wanted to believe him, but it was hard. She may appear selfish, like Tammy was the only one she cared about in this mess, but that wasn't true. She didn't like to think Daniel's brother was going through the same turmoil over this as well. Or that the homeless man had a family, maybe searching for him for months, wishing to save him from a life on the streets and the increased risk it brought. She nodded. "I'm sorry. I'm not trying to be difficult, but I'm so damn tired and frustrated."

The detective nodded. "With good reason. So tell us what happened here?"

"Not a lot to tell. Saul drove me home as I was still in shock after seeing the dead homeless man, realizing Tammy was connected, what with her locket in his possession. We got here and found the apartment like it is."

"Did you touch anything?"

She nodded. "I went to my room and packed a bag. I moved that kitchen chair. Other than that I haven't done a thing. The place is a mess."

The two policemen he came with wandered through the apartment. The detective continued with his questions. "I'm sure you've already discussed this, but maybe you can fill me in on any ideas you have as to what they would be looking for?"

She shook her head, all the fight gone. "No," she said softly. "I have no idea. Tammy didn't give me anything for safekeeping. I didn't think anything was wrong in her world, and I have no idea if she may or may not have left something here on purpose and how the bad guys thought I would have it."

"If somebody kidnapped her, looking for something she might've taken, it's only natural they would look at her best friend to see if she had passed it on," the detective said.

"No. That's faulty reasoning. She wouldn't put her best friend in danger."

"Unless you didn't know about it," Merk said.

"In which case, you'd be in more danger," the detective continued. "If she thought her place would be searched, she'd hide whatever it is somewhere else. Like here."

"In that case it could be anywhere, and it could mean whatever was here has already been found," Dakota suggested.

"As to what to look for—we are talking about a notebook, USB key, an SD card," Merk said.

She shook her head. "The options are way too numerous to even consider."

"We'll look around and see if we find anything," the detective told her.

She stood up and walked to the front door. "I'll sleep in my vehicle downstairs."

The detective turned to look at her. "Don't do that please."

She glared at him. "I don't have anywhere else to go."

"Go to a hotel for the night," the detective said, echoing Stone's earlier words. "Everything will look very different tomorrow."

Her gaze landed on the dill pickles and the top of the busted jar of mayonnaise. "It looks like shit no matter which way I see it."

She turned and walked out of her apartment. In the hallway, she pushed the button for the elevator. She didn't know why she was so resistant to a hotel. It was a reasonable answer. She could afford it. If it was just one night. Where else could she go? *Nowhere.* So why not do that? She figured it was one thing she could control amid a massive state of chaos she couldn't control. She was too damn tired to explore her psyche further or to drive too far. Plus what if the bad guys were following her or her car? She knew of no hotels or motels or bed-and-breakfasts in walking distance. Plus it was still dark outside.

The very circumstances Tammy had disappeared in.

She stepped into the elevator. Someone stepped on beside her. She shook her head. "You don't get tired of following me?"

"Not really. Some people need a little more babysitting than others."

She shot him a look. "You better not mean me. I didn't ask for any of this, and I'm doing the best I can to minimize the effect on others."

"True enough," he said cheerfully. "At the same time, loads of shit are going down. I can't get past the feeling that you must know more than you think you do."

"Then ask your questions because I have no idea what I might know."

"Did she give you any gifts in the last few months? Did she hand over something she wasn't using anymore but that you liked? Was there anything she bought for you?"

She shook her head. "No."

"That was a little too fast. At least think about it."

THE TROUBLE WAS, Saul knew she just wasn't in any kind of mental state to process what he said. He also knew, so often, girlfriends exchanged clothing, bits and pieces of household items and never thought anything of it. That was way too possible in this case as well. The girls appeared to be close to each other but no one else. He couldn't see Tammy deliberately hurting Rebel nor framing her. So maybe Tammy just needed a place to temporarily hide something where she knew it would be safe until she could come after it again.

He knew he was grasping at straws, but it was all they had at the moment. Nothing else made sense.

Downstairs he waited for her to catch up. She was dragging her feet, like she was ready to collapse in the car as soon as she got in. It would be a shame to wake her up when she didn't seem to be getting much quality sleep.

But he knew she'd have a much better sleep if she went to a hotel for the night. He grabbed the bag from her hand. "I'll carry it. You're too tired."

She didn't even argue, and that said a lot about where she was mentally. He understood. She'd had a rough week.

He knew Ice would have to tell Benji something soon, and so far there wasn't much to say. They found no sign of Daniel, no definitive answers as to what could have happened. Saul wasn't feeling exactly positive about the whole event either.

Too many scenarios were possible, and most of them didn't make Daniel come out as the good guy. Nor did it sound like he was alive, but Saul wasn't willing to guess on that one. He'd seen guys supposedly dead yet return alive many times. Just too much was going on here.

As they walked to the street, she pulled out her keys to unlock the vehicle and to prestart the car. He heard a strange shuffling sound. His mind reacted slower than his body. His body was already in motion, racing sideways, snatching her up and racing with her. He was around the side of the building before he stopped.

Gasping for breath she cried out, "What the hell was that about?"

He slipped his hand over her mouth and whispered, "Shh."

Above his hands her eyes opened wide. Then she nodded.

Sure now that she was committed, he released her and signaled that she stay behind him.

He wasn't sure what he'd heard, but it was too close to a sound he knew all too well—somebody coming in for an attack. The so-very-distinctive sound of footsteps in the grass. He waited but heard nothing further. He peered around the corner but didn't see anything. But he didn't trust his eyes or his ears.

The trouble was, his friends were still upstairs. If they came out, they could just as easily be taken by surprise. He pulled out his phone and texted them a warning. Having done that, he stilled for a long moment, waiting for noises, clues. When none came, he figured her stalker had left in the commotion of Saul moving Rebel to safety. He again motioned for her to stay where she was and then snuck around the corner, headed toward the front entrance to her apartment building.

Then remembered how two separate intruders had been at the warehouse.

He glanced back and saw her. Reassured, he jogged forward a few feet.

And the destruction to her apartment indicated more than just one guy had been there too.

He took another furtive look over his shoulder, glad, for once, that she kept poking her head around the corner, watching him.

If her car had been downstairs and locked in the parking garage, they would've gone to the basement. But, as it was, Saul hadn't known about the underground parking, so he had just parked on the street. The killer must have seen them arrive. That meant someone was watching the apartment or tracking her; either theory made sense. And, if the bad guy saw only one male exit the building with Rebel, maybe her stalker decided those were odds he could handle.

Saul found no sign of anyone lurking at the entrance-way. Feeling a little foolish, but aware his instincts were normally sound, he made his way back to her and said, "Come on. We can get out of here now." He unlocked the passenger door of her car and helped her inside.

Within seconds he was in the driver's side of the vehicle, pulling away from the building. As they left, he kept an eye out to see if anybody was on the grounds in the middle of the night. But he couldn't see anything. By the time he did reach the end of the block though, he knew why. A vehicle waited for them. Bright headlights shone in his rearview mirror.

In a low voice he muttered, "Shit."

She looked at him in alarm. "What do you mean, *shit?*"

"We're being followed."

She spun around to look out the back window. "Oh, my God. We have to lose them. We have to lose them," she cried out.

And, as that would be the best option, it certainly wasn't an easy one. The roads were deserted at this time in the early morning hours, and it would be hard to get ahead fast enough that the pursuers wouldn't see their taillights. He pulled his phone out, brought up his Contacts and tapped on the Stone icon.

When Stone answered, he said, "We picked up a tail as soon as we left the building."

"We're in the Jeep. Where are you?"

He waited a few seconds until he came to the next block and a street sign. "On Redding Road—we passed the corner of Balsa Street."

"Be there in five."

"I'm still moving, looking for a place to pull around and

maybe catch them. I see a hotel parking lot up ahead. If I can pull in there, maybe I can turn around in the parking lot and come up behind them."

"You're not very far ahead of us. No need to go without us."

"You got two minutes."

Saul laid the phone on the seat beside his leg and did several right turns, coming back up on the same street. He knew he couldn't lose his tail, but at least they knew he was on to them.

He slowed down to give his buddies a chance to catch up, the car tailing them slowing too. By then the hotel he had mentioned loomed ahead. He took a right at the corner and drove into the parking lot and around to the back. He was just ever-so-slightly ahead of his tail. It was a big hotel, and it was peak season, so there should be no shortage of vehicles in the rear parking area.

As soon as he rounded the corner into the parking lot, he killed the lights and drove slowly through the aisles of vehicles. At the very back he turned and waited. Almost instantly headlights came in behind him. He could feel the fear coming off Rebel beside him. "It'll be okay. Just take it easy."

She shook her head. "How can you guys do this all the time?"

"Ultimately what we do is helping people. We just happen to be particularly good at dishing out this kind of help."

"I'd rather bake cookies and deliver cupcakes," she muttered.

He let out a low bark of laughter. "There is a place in the world for that too."

"I think that's been the hardest thing about this whole

mess. I just feel so helpless."

"That's to be expected. We feel the same way. We have a lot of skills, but, if there's nothing to find, there is nothing to find. If we have no target, we have no one in particular to fight."

The vehicle came toward them again. Saul said, "Slide down to the bottom of the seat so your head is lower than the window. We don't want them to see us."

She crouched lower into her seat. He slid down so he could see out the topmost portion of the window. The vehicle drove down the aisle, went around beside them and back up along the far side.

He looked at her. "I would love to leave you here, locked in the vehicle, while I go after them."

She snorted. "Like that's safe for me."

"They didn't see you or even your vehicle parked here, and, if they don't know you're here, it might be safe. It would be worse for us if we let them get away. If I can at least get the license plate or, even better, stop them from leaving the parking lot, then we'll have actual suspects to question."

Just then another vehicle pulled into the parking lot.

He unlocked his door and said, "That's my Jeep. The rest of the guys are here. Lock the doors after me." He opened the door and stepped out, very quietly shutting the door behind him. And then he ran.

Chapter 10

REBEL WATCHED IN terror as Saul raced toward the Jeep, making hand signals.

The Jeep backed up and headed toward the other side of the parking lot. As if the stalkers understood they would get pinned in, the car sped up. But the Jeep had more power under the hood and jumped forward into the car's path. They just barely avoided a collision as the car hit the brakes and squealed to a stop.

But the driver hit Reverse immediately and backed up fast to put as much space between him and the Jeep as he could.

She couldn't see everything that was happening, and all she could think of was them getting run over in the dark. The air filled with danger. She desperately wanted to leave her vehicle. The confined space was suffocating. What if someone saw her? Instead she followed instructions—for the second time in a row tonight, yet the first time in a long time—and stayed put. The headlights were going crazy on the far side. Someone raced in her direction on foot. It was too dark to see who it was.

She waited until he got closer. As he ran past her car, he turned right in between the vehicle she was in and the car next to hers. She unlocked her passenger door, choosing her time well, and threw open the door right into his body, slamming him hard. She was out and on him in an instant. She pinned him to the ground and landed one fist against his chin, the second against his nose. She would take care of this asshole before he took care of anybody else.

Only she was not an even match for this asshole on the ground. He flipped her off his chest. But she hung on. It was awkward, still prone on the concrete parking lot, confined between two vehicles. She couldn't get any decent blows in, and she couldn't get her legs to work properly. Pissed but exhausted, the shocks kept coming as she resorted to hitting him, blindly kicking, slamming anything she could to knock this man back down and keep him down. Suddenly hands grasped around her ribs and lifted her.

"Take it easy, Rebel," Saul said. "Take it easy. It's all right. We've got him."

Slowly she let her body relax in his arms as she realized several other men had grabbed the man, hauling him to his feet out from between the vehicles.

"Thank God," she whispered.

He held her back against his chest, her arms and hands still clutched in his arms crisscrossed about her body. She watched them cuff the man's hands behind him and zip-tied his feet, then propped the man up against her car. Flashlights on, they moved so she could look at his face. Although battered and bleeding, his features were quite distinctive. And unfortunately they were also completely foreign to her.

"I have no idea who he is," she said. She pushed away from Saul to see the stranger better. "What the hell are you doing following us?"

He glared at her. "We weren't following you. Why the hell did you try to beat the crap out of me?"

She sneered. "So you can tell your buddies you were

beaten up by a girl."

"No, I'll tell them I was attacked by psychobitch."

She laughed. "If I find out you had anything to do with Tammy's disappearance, asshole, I'll make sure you're this psychobitch's victim."

He struggled to free himself, but Saul slammed him back against the car.

She glanced over at the other men. "What about the other person in the car? Or was this asshole alone?"

"We got him. He's unconscious." Merk motioned to the side.

She turned to see the massive hulk of Stone carrying another man by his right arm alone, his hand gripping the belt around her stalker's waist. She stared at the man, his feet dragging on the ground, and shook her head. Under her breath she whispered, "Jesus." She stared up at Stone, but he gave her a bland look. She shuddered and stepped closer to Saul.

He chuckled. "Stone never hurts anyone who doesn't need it."

"I'm glad to hear that." She stared again at the asshole in front of her. "Did you have anything to do with Tammy's disappearance?"

The man sneered but kept his mouth shut.

"You want me to set Stone on you?" she asked, her voice rising.

"You guys can't touch me. You're all about that law-abiding-citizen bullshit."

She sneered right back. "Maybe they are, but I'm not." She did a hop-jump kick and caught him in the gut.

He bent over double, his face turning white.

She slammed her hands against his shoulders to hold

him upright again. "Asshole."

He gasped for air. "You're a fucking bitch. You'll pay for that."

She was just going to let that slide, turning to walk away. Instead she took two steps, turned and, with her left foot, shot out and kicked him across the jaw. That surprise quieted him for a bit. "Yeah, a sneak attack with your crew would be your style to take on one woman," she snapped. "You wouldn't come at me in the dark without a bunch of idiot muscle beside you. Is that what you fucking did to Tammy?" When he remained silent—glaring, but silent—she shook her head, grabbed him by the ear and twisted hard. When he yelped, she shoved her face into his and said, "Tell me about Tammy."

"I didn't touch her." He saw her pull her leg back and yelled, "No wait. I know the guys who snatched her."

Rebel straightened and leaned forward. "Where is she?"

He shook his head. "I don't know where they took her."

"Who took her?" Saul asked.

The man shook his head. "Look, I was just told to keep an eye on you guys and on the bitch."

"Why?"

"The boss said so, that's why."

"Who's the boss, and what was he looking for?"

"I'm not saying who my boss is. But he said, if she came out with anything in her hand, to grab her."

"Is that what you were doing tonight?" Saul asked.

He nodded. "She came out with a bag in her hand. I don't know if it's what the boss wanted or not."

She stepped back and crossed her arms over her chest. She had more ideas about how to get the information she wanted out of him. Before she could start in on the man again, Saul grabbed the stooge by the back of the neck and said quietly, "I suggest you start being a little more forthcoming."

"Hey, look, I just told you something."

"What about Daniel?" Stone asked.

The man shook his head. "The same person who took Tammy took Daniel."

"And what about the man whose throat was cut," Merk said, his voice hard.

The man stared from one face to the other.

When his eyes landed on Rebel, she beamed a big smile at him. "You better talk," she said, "or else …"

He glared at her. "You can't just beat me up. That's brutality."

"I'm not a cop. But I am the woman whose apartment was totally trashed, and you just admitted to knowing about the kidnapping of two people and likely sliced that poor man's throat, all on your own."

"I did not," he yelled. He motioned at the guy Stone still carried around. "Carney here did that."

"Interesting." She turned to look at the unconscious man. "Don't let go of that asshole."

Stone opened his hand. The man dropped to the ground, and Stone put his foot on the man's back. He crossed his arms and stared at their conscious prisoner. "Who took Daniel and Tammy?"

The prisoner shrugged but was quick to look at the ground. "I don't know. I didn't have nothing to do with any of it."

"What are you? Just the lookout?"

The man nodded. "Something like that. I screwed up another job, so I was downgraded to keep watch."

"And vandalizing my property?"

He faced her. "Rich bitch like you probably got insurance anyway."

She snorted. "Like that makes a difference."

"You have any idea what your boss is looking for?" Stone asked.

He shook his head. "Not a clue."

"So then why did they take Tammy?" Saul asked.

"She had something that didn't belong to her."

"Oh, no you don't," Rebel snapped. "Don't you dare make her out to be a bad guy."

"She got it at her job. I don't know any more than that."

Rebel stepped back. "Saul, maybe you are right then."

He nodded slowly. "What about Daniel?"

"No idea, but he was marked for quite a while. They were just waiting for him to complete something, see if he had any further use. Like everything else they do, when they're done, they take out the garbage."

"Are Daniel and Tammy alive?" Merk asked.

The prisoner looked at Merk hesitantly. And then nodded. "I think so. But I can't be too sure."

"How will we find them?"

He motioned to the unconscious man on the ground. "Through him. I don't know where they are."

Rebel studied his face, the smirk slipping in and out of his features. "I'm not sure I believe you."

"I don't have any reason to lie," he protested.

She snorted. "Anything to save your sorry ass."

He shrugged. "I don't want to get into trouble, but I'm already in trouble. The thing is, I didn't have anything to do with that guy's death, and I didn't have anything to do with the kidnappings."

"But you did know about them, so that makes you just as guilty in the eyes of the law," Merk said.

"No, I only knew about them afterward. I didn't have anything to do with it myself. I only heard when Carney here was bragging about it today."

"Why would they have kept Daniel and Tammy alive?" she asked quietly. That bugged her. There had to be a reason. Because otherwise they would've killed them right away.

"Because the kidnappers needed their help to be sure they could access the information they stole."

"Both of them?"

He shrugged. "Leverage for the other."

Rebel gasped. "Now that sounds like the truth." She glared at him, took a step toward him, her fist already forming. She reached back only to have Saul grab her hand.

He whispered to her, "As much as you might want to, and he might deserve it, we don't want added trouble. The cops are on the way. We'll let them handle it."

"And if the cops are involved?"

Saul sent her a hard look. "We will believe the cops are *not* involved, thank you."

She shrugged off his restraining arm. "Fine. But it's not my fault if he accidentally trips on the way to the cop car." She shot the prisoner a hard look and stepped back.

Saul was right, but she hated to admit it. It was one thing to beat up the man to get the information they needed. But now that he was cooperating, she didn't have too much justification for pounding his face into the concrete. No matter how much she wanted to.

Unfortunately.

SAUL LIKED THESE new developments. He stared at the man flat out on the parking lot. In typical Stone fashion, he'd knocked out this guy so he wouldn't get in the way while they caught the second man. But that also meant the asshole wouldn't wake up anytime soon.

And that was too bad. "We need to talk to the unconscious man."

"Not happening." Rebel groaned. "Unless you have cold water to throw in his face."

Saul looked from one man to the other. Then he leaned over and squeezed a spot on the man's neck.

Almost instantly the man groaned.

Saul gave a thin smile.

From beside him, Rebel said in a low tone, "Cool trick. I need to learn that one."

He shook his head. "It doesn't always work, so it's not something you can count on."

She nodded. "Still I'm grateful for it right now."

When the man opened his eyes, he stared up at Rebel and the circle of men surrounding him, confused, shocked and then angry.

"Glad to see you're back with us," Saul said calmly. "Now we'll get some answers from you."

"I'm not saying nothing."

"It doesn't matter if you do or not, your cohort already has," Rebel said.

The man glared at Rebel, then twisted to see if his buddy was still around. Saul stepped in front of the one man so they couldn't see each other. "You won't be talking to him anytime soon."

"I'm not talking to anybody." He closed his eyes and lay on the ground. "I'll have my lawyer sue you for assaulting me."

"We'll see how that works in the courts. Where the hell is Tammy?"

"And Daniel," Stone said, his voice hard. He nudged the man with his foot. "I packed you over here. I'm quite happy to pack you over to that bridge beside us and drop you off the edge."

The man's eyes snapped open. He glared as if deliberating whether Stone was serious or not. But the look on Stone's face made him say, "I don't know anything."

"You're lying," Saul said quietly. "We already know you picked up Tammy and Daniel."

The man's face twisted in disgust. "You don't believe that snitch, do you? The boss kicked him down a peg because he was such a screw-up."

"Well, in this case, he'll probably get kicked down another peg for tattling on you."

"They'll kill him for screwing up again."

"That's the thing, you see? He'd do anything to save his ass."

"What will you say to save yours?" Rebel snapped.

He glared at her. "I'm not talking to you at all, bitch."

"Were you part of that mess in my apartment?"

Understanding whispered across his face, then he sneered. "I was looking for something."

"Yeah, did you find it?"

His face turned suspicious. "No. But, if you have it, that might be a good bargaining tool for you."

Saul glanced at Stone, then to Merk and Dakota. He knew what they were all thinking. It *would* be a bargaining chip. Too bad they didn't have it.

The trouble was, Rebel had a mind of her own.

"And if I do, do I get Tammy back?"

"And Daniel," Stone added.

She shrugged. "Okay, him too."

The man on the ground gave a bark of laughter. "Nice to see you don't like him either."

"I care about Tammy. They care about Daniel. Between us, we want the pair of them back," she snapped. She reached out and kicked him in the foot. "Now talk."

He shook his head. "Nope, I want to see the key first."

"Why would I show you anything? So you can get a message to the rest of your cohorts? So they can come after me?"

"They will anyway."

She shoved her hands deeper into her pockets as if hiding something and surreptitiously studied him watching her.

Saul understood what she was doing, but she was playing a dangerous game. He walked around to stand behind her, giving her the show of their support.

The man's gaze rose to study the hard faces surrounding him, and he shrugged. "All I can do is tell the boss you have it. He might arrange a barter."

"This is a risky business you're in."

"No, not me. You got in the middle of something you aren't sure about. Chances are you won't all walk away from this with your lives. Think carefully before you take this step."

"Or we could just torture you to get the information out of you." Rebel looked at Stone. "Did you happen to take his ID and everything else off him before you dropped him?" Stone reached into his pocket and pulled out the man's wallet. She held out her hand. "Let's see who he is, where he lives. We can probably run down all the places he's been to the last week quite easily."

"If you start playing games, they will shoot you before they ever take care of anything. They can take the key off a dead body just as easily as off a live one. Actually easier."

The other prisoner made a strangled sound.

Seeing the understanding in their eyes, Saul realized, in their minds, this would likely only have one outcome. "We can play hardball too."

"But all we want is Tammy and Daniel back safe and sound and to be left alone," Rebel jumped in.

"Then you better have the goddamn key, and it better have the information on it the boss needs."

"I have no idea what's on it. I haven't looked." Rebel stood casually. She answered like a pro.

Saul admired her, but, at the same time, he was worried that she had more guts than brains.

"You have to let us go so I can arrange a meeting."

Merk snorted. "Call your boss and arrange a meeting right now."

Stone held out the man's phone. "Make the call."

He slowly sat up, reached for the phone, hit Contacts, pushed on a name and made a call. "They want to make a bargain. The two hostages for the key."

At something the other man said, he looked up. "There are five of them here. They got the two of us surrounded."

Saul wished the damn thing was on Speakerphone. And he wanted the contact information off that asshole's phone. Stone had been slow to bring the man over, so Saul didn't know if Stone got what he could off of it. It hadn't been on the top of their priority list, considering they still needed to grab the second man.

"One hour. Okay, we can do that." The man tucked his

phone into his pocket defiantly until Stone retrieved it. "He says one hour, back where you were earlier."

"At the warehouse where you slit the poor man's throat?" Rebel snapped. "Why the hell would I go back there with you?"

"He was in the wrong place at the wrong time. Besides, he was messing in something that wasn't his business."

"You mean, Tammy's locket of course."

At that comment he was oddly silent. The man glared at her. "You know too fucking much, bitch."

She shrugged. Obviously she had hit a nerve. Maybe he would be demoted now for leaving behind evidence of Tammy that connected her to that warehouse. "Maybe. Maybe I just don't know enough yet. That's all right. I'll keep digging until I do."

"You'll find a bullet between your eyes for all your troubles." He shook his head and hopped to his feet. Instantly the men tensed. "We have to get down there. Otherwise our boss won't show."

He turned and looked around the parking lot. "Where the fuck is my car?"

Merk motioned to the other side. "It's back there."

"If we're not there on time, we're all getting a bullet."

No doubting the man's sincerity this time.

"We can't just let him leave," Rebel said. "Can you at least blow his kneecaps apart or something? So that he doesn't take off on us?"

The man spun. "You watch it. That might just be you next time. When a deal happens, a deal happens. This is either done properly, or it doesn't go down. You guys can follow me back to the warehouse. But, in the meantime, I'm getting into my car and driving to the rendezvous." He glanced over at his buddy and said, "Pete, come on. Let's get the hell out of here. You know the boss will take care of this."

As the two men left, Saul turned to stare at the others, then asked, "She's right. What the hell are we doing here?"

"Going to a meeting apparently," Rebel said tiredly.

"They have Tammy and Daniel, so we can't just let him go," Saul reminded her.

She nodded. "Okay. I'll do whatever we can to bring her back." She rolled her eyes at Stone. "Yes, Daniel too. I still don't like the idea of them heading off alone," she muttered.

"I put a tracker on the vehicle," Stone said. "We can find them wherever."

"Really?" She brightened. "Did you copy his phone contacts?" she asked hopefully.

He shook his head. But then he grinned. "I took pictures of them all instead."

For the first time, her smile was genuine.

Chapter 11

REBEL LET SAUL drive. She trusted his driving. The other guys were in the Jeep. She was so damn close to finding Tammy that she was terrified something would go wrong at the last minute. "What if they were lying?"

"Good question." He glanced at her. "The problem is, they want the key, and we have no idea where it is."

"I might have one here we can use as a decoy. It'll give us a little bit of time—maybe about five minutes, if they have a laptop with them."

She shuffled through the glove box, not finding anything. She looked through her purse, pulled out a small one. "This is one I use daily."

No doubt what it was. "Is that it? You carry USB keys with you?"

"Often, yes. I do marketing. I often bring work home. Nothing on this is confidential. It's all work-in-progress."

"Good thing. We can use that to stall them—at least for a few minutes."

He pointed to the USB key sitting in one of the cup-holders. "Is that another one?"

She reached for it. "Well, it's a USB key, but it's not mine."

He turned to look at her. "Whose is it?"

"It has no identifying marks on it. It's just a generic purple plastic one." She sank back. "Purple," she whispered.

"What?"

"Tammy has all things in purple."

"You think it could be hers?"

"Maybe. Why would she have left it here? By accident?"

"Or by design."

She turned to him. "What if she did leave this for me? Or left it here for security?" She looked around the car. "But it's hardly secure."

"Then again it's something people would overlook. Do you normally keep your vehicle clean?"

She nodded. "All the time. Usually weekly. I just cleaned it out a couple weeks ago, before my life got crazy. I didn't see it then."

"When was she last in your vehicle?"

"I'm not sure." She cast her mind back, figuring out an answer to that question, but she wasn't getting anywhere. She shook her head. "At least a few days before she went missing."

"Even if you saw the key, you probably never thought anything about."

She nodded. "I've done that before," she admitted. "I wish I had my laptop with me. If you have one, we should check this out. I don't want to give them the stuff that they want. I don't know what this is. Maybe it's proof somebody at the company is stealing? Or doing something criminal?"

"So maybe we'll give them yours, and we'll keep this one hidden somewhere safe." He pulled out his phone and called Stone.

She looked at him. She was never a fan of phone calls and driving at the same time. Only he seemed to have no problem.

"Stone, we found the key hidden in her car. We don't have a laptop here to check it out. Do you have one there?"

"Merk has his."

"We need to meet up somewhere so we can figure out what's going on here. This USB key happens to be purple, which is Tammy's favorite color."

"Yes, quite a few purple knickknacks were at her place. We need a decoy key to give them."

"We have one." Saul turned to look at Rebel. "Rebel found one in her purse."

"Okay, good. We may need to give them the real key, but let's copy the information off it first."

"Do we have time?" Rebel asked. "We can't afford to be late."

The men quickly organized a meeting place, and Saul pulled into a parking lot—a block away from the warehouse, at the back of the grocery store—and parked off to the side. Within seconds the Jeep pulled up beside him and parked. Saul and Rebel got out and walked toward the Jeep. Rebel could see the laptop powering up on Stone's lap.

Saul motioned to Rebel. "Give Stone Tammy's key."

"Can't guarantee it is Tammy's," she said. "It just happens to not be mine."

"Good." Stone docked the key to the laptop and opened up a couple Excel documents. "Accounts? Beyond that it is just gibberish."

"Well, it means something to somebody," Saul said. "Which makes it important."

"Right."

Rebel watched Stone copy the contents and send it to somebody. "Who did you send it to? That's confidential information."

"I sent it to my boss," Stone said quietly. "We have several accounting specialists at our place. All trustworthy. All security conscious. Someone will decipher what's going on here. And we need to know about that so we understand what the hell kind of trouble Tammy has gotten herself into."

"Well let's hope by the time they figure it out, we've already solved the case."

Saul checked his watch. "We can use the other key and give them just enough for them to be satisfied. We'll keep this one so they don't get their hands on it. We're almost out of time. Let's head down and make sure we arrive on the spot in time."

"I'd rather be early," Rebel said. "And I wish we had more men, just in case the bad guys come with a lot of extra manpower. We could be outnumbered."

Saul glanced at her and smiled. "You don't trust us," he teased.

She shook her head. "I trust you guys. It's them I don't trust." On that cryptic note, she walked over to the passenger side of her car and got in.

"She's got a point," Saul said.

The men nodded.

"Where is their car right now?" Merk asked.

Stone opened a different program, twisted it slightly so the others could see. "They've stopped at an address here," he said. "I just contacted the detective and shared that info. He'll get backup to us immediately. Told him what we're doing, where we're at and where to find the vehicle."

"They could be making a pit stop," Dakota said, a knowing smile on his face. "We did do a good job of scaring the crap out of them."

"Or," Saul said, on a more serious note, "they could have stopped in the same warehouse district but by that series of abandoned buildings."

"Maybe a visit with the boss?" Stone asked.

"I suggest we drive by first and see," Merk said.

"I'll follow you." Saul smacked the outside of the Jeep. "Everybody get moving. We don't have time to waste." He got into the driver's side of Rebel's car as the Jeep roared to life, reversed and headed out onto the street. He watched his vehicle go and smiled. He loved that thing.

"What's the smile for?"

"That's my Jeep." There was a little bit of pride in his voice. "I left it here when I initially moved to Texas."

"How come they're driving your Jeep and not you?"

"My focus right now is on taking care of you." In his mind, it was that simple. If he could have gotten her into the Jeep with the rest of the guys, that would've been easier. He'd still have to take care of her then too. He smiled.

"They will damage it."

The smile fell off his face. "That's just a mean and cruel thought."

She chuckled. "Can you tell me it's never been in an accident or shot at yet?"

He shrugged. "Okay, it has been. I was hoping to drive it back to Texas this trip, but I need several days off to make the long drive. It's been parked at my mother's house, but I might leave it at a friend's place when I fly out this time."

"Nice friend."

Saul nodded. "The father of one of our bosses. We stay with him regularly when we're out West."

"Nice." She wished she had more people to draw on in times like this.

They hit the warehouse district after another five minutes. "Aren't we going to the same warehouse first?" she asked.

He turned to look at her. "No, the other vehicle with Carney and Pete stopped here and hasn't moved since."

She nodded. "As long as they don't see us," she warned.

"That's the plan."

Saul drove ahead, slowing down as he approached the GPS location. He killed the lights on the car and slowly drove forward. The car sat parked at the front of a warehouse that looked deserted as hell.

"Aww, shit," he said under his breath.

"What do you see?"

"I don't see anything or anyone."

"So why *aww, shit?*"

"Because I don't like this." He pulled in and headed around the back. As they moved forward, she saw no lights anywhere in the building. And she knew the inside of that warehouse would be deserted.

Saul pulled up to Stone who stood beside the Jeep, his phone out, talking to someone. Saul rolled down his window and spoke to Merk, standing beside Stone. "And?"

Merk turned a grim face in his direction. "One bullet hole between the eyes for each of them."

"Goddamnit."

Rebel reached over and grabbed his hand. "What does that mean about the meeting? Does that mean they won't be there?"

"It means these two won't be there," Merk said. "Now we're dealing with the unknown. And that's not a twist I like."

She closed her eyes and slumped into her seat, her hands

fisted.

Saul gently wrapped his much larger hand around one of her fists. "Easy. Somebody will still show up. We have the key."

"Why don't we just give them the real key?" Rebel asked. "We already have a copy. It doesn't make any difference. Let them have the real one, and let's just get our people back."

She watched as he got out of the vehicle and walked over to talk to the men. With the windows down, she could almost decipher the conversation. They were so close to finding Tammy that she could hardly breathe. If Rebel lost this lead, chances were good she'd never save her friend. As much as she didn't want her two stalkers dead, she was glad for the information they'd gotten from them first.

She tried to swallow a sob caught in the back of her throat. The abandoned warehouse might appear to be silent and empty, but that didn't mean it was. The last thing she wanted was a bullet between her eyes—or Tammy's. But she also knew their time was running out.

Just then Saul hopped back in the vehicle. "We will give them the key because, like you said, we have a copy. It's our best chance of convincing them we have what they want. The problem then becomes, since they *will* have what they want, they don't need us or Tammy or Daniel anymore."

"What about Detective Wilson?"

"He'll meet us there."

She gave a strangled laugh. "If he makes it on time."

Saul shook his head. "Take it easy. He's doing the best he can. They'll probably be an extra five or ten minutes, but that's it. They know how important this is to their case too."

She nodded, but she didn't feel like agreeing to anything.

When Saul started the vehicle and drove out slowly, she wanted to yell at him to hit the gas and get to the meeting. She wanted to scream with frustration but finally gasped out, "Why are you driving so slowly?"

"Because the guys and I want to see who and what might be wandering around this part of town."

Logical, reasonable and it didn't make a bit of difference to her. "I don't see how you can see anything out there. It's so damn dark out."

She barely recognized the area even though she'd been here earlier. When he drove into the warehouse parking lot and parked the car, almost at the exact same spot she'd parked in before, she breathed a sigh of relief. Without giving him a chance to stop her, she hopped out and quietly closed the car door. She listened, her head tilted toward the inside of the building. The area appeared deserted. Saul got out, walked around to her side. Instead of looking at the building he searched high above.

"What you are looking for?"

He turned toward her, then whispered, "Snipers."

Her heart froze. How the hell would she handle that? She had no idea what all she could be up against right now. And these men were so much better prepared than she was. It was a daunting thought how she'd been coming close to smacking into this very situation anytime in the last week. Plus, if any of these men had caught her, she'd become a hostage, just like the rest. Or worse, she'd be dead just like the two men they'd killed just moments ago.

He reached out and grabbed her hand. "Stay with me. Stay silent. Do not, under any circumstances, separate from me. Do you understand?"

She nodded. "I understand." She turned to look around

for the other men, realizing the Jeep hadn't showed up. She squeezed his hand and walked toward the building. "Where are the others?"

"They're already here."

She let out her breath gently. Just because she couldn't see them, it didn't mean they hadn't arrived.

He squeezed her hand in reassurance and slowly walked her toward to the front of the building. "Have you got the key?"

She lifted it in her fingers.

He nodded. "Good."

They stepped inside the building. This vast monstrosity of glass and tin was deserted, desolate. Shivers ran down her back. How she wanted to run home. But, if Tammy was here, no way would Rebel turn tail and run. She thrust her chin forward and glared at the building that terrified her. Things would likely get so much worse tonight. She had to keep a handle on her emotions before Saul sent her back to the vehicle and insisted she stay locked in there. That was the last thing she wanted to do.

With him leading her, they slowly and silently searched the bottom of the building and then took the stairs. She knew they would end up in the room where the homeless man had been killed. It made sense that, somewhere along the line, Tammy had been here.

Upstairs, still walking quietly, Saul led her in the direction where the homeless man had been found. Just before entering, he stopped and listened, his head leaning to one side. He squeezed her hand, and, in a low voice, almost soundless against her ear, he whispered, "They're here. Be prepared."

She stiffened and gripped his fingers like a lifeline.

He stepped around the doorway.

In the shadows of the darkness, a man said, "Step inside."

Saul took a step forward, dragging her with him.

She tried to see in the darkness, not even the moonlight allowed inside. She could see shapes on the ground, but she didn't know who or what they were.

"Did you bring it?"

An owl hooted close by, making her shiver at the lonely sound. "Yes," she said defiantly. "Where's Tammy?" Remembering the look from Stone, she added, "And Daniel."

"You'll get them as soon as I can check the merchandise." A soft glow came from a laptop as it opened.

Saul took the key from her hand, took four steps forward and held it out.

A man detached from the shadows. She didn't recognize him. He took the key from Saul's hand and walked over to the man with the laptop.

Saul stood beside her again. Instinctively she reached out for his hand. No way could she stop him from feeling the shivers racking her body. She was so damned scared.

Silence reigned while the key was inserted, and the documents opened. Then the laptop was closed, and they were ordered, "Turn around, and stand in the doorway."

She gasped. "Where's Tammy? You promised us Tammy was here."

"Turn around, and stand in the doorway," the man said again. His tone told them that no arguments were allowed.

She heard guns cocking, and she realized she finally may have hit the end of the road with her own reckless actions. At Saul's urging, she stepped into the doorway with him. And she waited.

For the bullet that would end her life.

SAUL KNEW THE guys wouldn't be far away. He could only hope they were in the room already. There had been another hallway, leading to other rooms. He squeezed Rebel's hand, and, in as low a voice as he could, he whispered, "Get ready." He felt her stare of surprise and whispered, "Three, two and one."

She was jerked to the left. He pulled her all the way to him and out the doorway into the hall. He listened for footsteps; none came. She stared at him in surprise. He held a finger to his lips. And then he heard the hoot of an owl again. He relaxed.

He motioned back to the room and said, "Now to call Stone."

She stared at him with wide eyes. "What?"

He led her back into the dark room, almost having to push her, she was so resistant. And then they heard it again. An owl. Only this time it was super close. She gasped as a flashlight turned on.

"It's okay, Rebel. It's us."

Saul stared into the faces of Saul's men, then dropped his gaze to the floor. "Did you get them?"

"We got two of them. One of them has disappeared."

"What about Tammy?" She raced forward. "Where's Tammy?"

The flashlight moved through the room, but nobody else was here.

She spun and stared at Saul. "We have to find her."

Saul shared hard glances with Stone. They both knew the chances of either hostage being handed over was minimal.

"What was that?" Rebel cried out. She turned and raced out.

"Wait," Saul called out.

But she was gone.

Swearing, he darted from the room behind her. And then he heard what she'd heard.

A woman sobbing.

The others heard it too. With flashlights shining in front of them, they searched the top floor. "Rebel, where are you?"

"I'm downstairs."

"Damn woman." Saul raced after her, knowing the men would finish searching upstairs and then make their way downstairs.

Rebel screamed.

"What? Wait for me," he roared.

"No, it's okay," she cried out, laughing and crying as he got closer. "It's Tammy. She's alive. I found her."

Chapter 12

REBEL DROPPED BESIDE her friend.

The woman moaned, her sob deep, guttural.

"Easy, Tammy. Take it easy. Help is coming."

The woman made a small head movement and groaned again.

Rebel could hear the men coming toward her.

"Over here," she said. "Bring a flashlight."

Instantly light shone in her direction and then fell on the woman, first on her face, then at her feet.

"Oh, my God," Rebel said.

"What?" Saul said, dropping to his knees beside her. "What does that mean?"

"It's not Tammy." Her heart stricken, Rebel stared down at the female supervisor Tammy had never got along with. "This is Samantha, Daniel's and Tammy's boss."

"Well, I guess that answers a few more questions." Saul reached out and touched the woman's pulse. "She's been badly beaten, and her pulse is thready."

Blood was everywhere. Her leg was obviously broken. Her breath came out in short gasps. Saul said, "Broken ribs, possibly a punctured lung too."

Stone came up behind them. "The ambulance is on its way. We're taking a quick look around, inside and out, to make sure Daniel and Tammy aren't here as well."

Rebel heard them, but she was so shocked she couldn't have spoken if she'd tried. She reached down to the woman's hand, hearing her groan in pain. She backed off and whispered, "Oh, my God! What have they done to her?"

"Probably broke almost every bone in her body," Saul said, fatigue and wariness in his face. "We see stuff like this with drug deals that have gone bad. Although nowadays they usually just put a bullet in you. A beating like this is very personal and usually as a warning to others."

"And Tammy? Does that mean they've done worse to her?"

He lifted his gaze and studied Rebel. "Keep hoping, remember? We don't know where or how Tammy is." He motioned at Samantha and asked, "Any idea how long she's been missing?"

Rebel shook her head. "No, I've been out of the loop most of this last week."

Worry about finding Tammy was all Rebel could do besides whispering encouragement to the poor woman. Samantha was in such a bloody mess. Rebel wanted to pat her arm or squeeze her hand or give her a hug, but she didn't dare touch Samantha for fear of hurting her further. It was such a relief to hear the ambulance's wailing siren in the distance. Surely the cops were coming too. Like where was the detective? Mentally she willed them to get here faster. Anything to help this woman.

At the same time, she was desperate to search more of this building to hopefully find Tammy. "Why would they have brought Samantha and not the others?"

Saul didn't say anything for a long moment.

She took a wild guess. "Because they could. Because they held all the cards. Because Samantha was still alive, and the others are dead."

"They could still have brought the others even if they were dead."

"It's also possible," Merk added, "that they wanted to make sure they have exactly what they need on the key, or they may need more information from Tammy and Daniel before they kill them."

"And yet, we found out nothing further. We don't know where Tammy and Daniel are, and the vehicle we tracked here only led us to the pair of dead men. The asshole who took our friends is gone in the wind yet again."

The truth was so damn painful she didn't know how to handle it. She wanted to scream in rage, and yet, she wanted to curl up in a corner, defeated. As she stared down at the poor broken woman in front of her, she realized Tammy didn't have a hope in hell.

Rebel reached out a trembling hand, brushing back a couple strands of the woman's hair and heard a heavy gurgling sound followed by silence. As in all-the-way silent. Rebel gasped, her hand covering her mouth as she frantically waited for the woman's chest to rise yet again.

But it didn't.

"Oh, no, no, no, no. Please breathe. Please breathe."

Saul grabbed her hand. "Stay steady."

She raised dripping eyes to him and whispered, "She's dead."

"Yes. But I don't think any of us could have done anything for her in the meantime. She was very badly injured."

Just then uniformed men, police burst through the door. EMTs came running to the body. Saul stood, stepped around the body and pulled Rebel out of the way. The EMTs went to work.

As she watched, she kept up hope. "She just stopped breathing," she cried out. "Please try to save her."

The men didn't seem to hear. They were so focused on the woman in front of them. They worked on her heart, trying to keep it pumping, but ten minutes later they shook their heads.

Rebel burst into tears—her heart hurting and the fear in her mind growing by the second. She was tucked up against a warm chest.

Saul wrapped his arms around her and held her close. He just held her; he didn't rub her back or arms. He didn't share any platitudes this time.

She was ready to implode, like a hurricane was inside her, drawing everything inward. She cried, hating the sense of weakness that was desperate for a release from the constant tension inside.

When the worst elements of the storm blew over, she stood quietly in the circle of Saul's arms, wondering if there was something more she could've done to save the woman.

Saul gently stroked her hair from her face. "What can I do to help you right now?"

She rubbed her eyes with her sleeve, like a two-year-old. She stepped back but didn't look at him. "Sorry about that," she muttered. "I haven't broken down like that in a long time."

"It's to be expected. Don't be too hard on yourself. You've had a series of shocks, culminating in what we thought was relief, only to find defeat instead."

She lifted her gaze to stare at him dully. "I don't even know what to do now."

"You need to sleep. We all do."

She looked around. "Did the others find anybody else?"

He shook his head. "No."

She bowed her head. "Tammy's dead, isn't she?"

Saul didn't answer.

SAUL DIDN'T WANT to answer. Because, if Tammy wasn't already dead, chances were she'd soon wish she was. In his mind he couldn't come up with one reason for keeping Tammy and Daniel alive. Samantha was so badly beaten. This asshole was responsible for two kidnappings and four deaths now.

Stone walked toward them, motioning at the police all around them and asked, "Ready to go?"

He nodded. "Where to?"

"To the police station. Of the two men we caught, one was shot. The EMTS will take him into custody and take him to the hospital, but the other one is heading to the station. Neither had IDs on them."

Saul nodded. He remembered the mention of catching the men, but he sure as hell didn't remember most of the details after handing over the key. It all had moved so damn fast afterward. That they had two live men to question, well, that made him feel like cheering. "I sure hope we get a chance to question them after the police do," he said. "After what they did to that woman …"

Stone nodded, his gaze hard. "Don't worry. Even if he makes it to jail, he won't live long."

"Still too damn long," Rebel said passionately. "They broke her to pieces."

Saul wrapped an arm around her shoulders and tucked her close again. "That doesn't mean the same thing was done to Tammy."

Rebel took a deep shaky breath and then let it out slowly. "I keep hanging on to that."

"We have work to do, but we also need some rest. Police station it is, then back to Richard's to crash. A fresh start in the morning."

"Sounds good to me." Saul led Rebel away from the bloody stains on the floor, outside toward her car.

She moved automatically, her face blank with exhaustion. She got in the vehicle when he told her to, sat and buckled up. And she hadn't said anything. She just stared, her arms wrapped around her chest. He closed her door, walked around to the driver's side and, in a low voice, he said to Stone, "She's in bad shape."

Merk joined them. "I just told Foster that she'll come home with us. If nothing else, it gives her a place to stay for the night."

Saul nodded. "I'll follow you guys." He got into her vehicle, started the engine, waited for the Jeep to pull out and then slipped behind it into the empty street. He heard her small voice.

"Where are we going?"

"First to the police station, then some place safe to get some sleep."

"And me?"

"You'll stay with us for the moment."

Her relief was palpable.

He reached over and gently curled her fingers into his hand and squeezed. "We won't leave you."

"You guys are here on a job. For me this is my life. If I don't find Tammy, I don't know how I can even begin to start over."

He squeezed her fingers again and dropped her hand as

he put both hands back on steering wheel, shifting gears as he turned the corner and headed up Main Street. "We have to remember that was not Tammy. Maybe that's a good sign. Maybe it's not. What we do know is, Tammy could still be alive."

She settled back and closed her eyes. "Why the police station?"

"Merk and Dakota have brought along the two men they captured. One was shot by his boss. The bullet didn't go between his eyes like the others. It grazed one side of the skull. I suspect he'll be okay, but we know he's gone under guard to the hospital."

She opened her eyes. "We got someone?" She half sat up. "Two someones?"

He nodded and explained.

When she collapsed in relief, her fervent whisper was, "Thank God, that's huge."

"I know, right? It's not a total loss."

"We should have questioned them before the cops came. Otherwise we can't make them tell us what we want to know."

He chuckled. "I trust Stone."

"Is he the one who found them?"

Saul nodded.

She grinned. "Then let's hope Stone is every bit as mean as he looks."

"They are all teddy bears. Stone is just the biggest of the lot."

"So many of those big guys are," she whispered.

"Let's just get through the police station visit, and then we can get some rest. A few hours' sleep will make a hell of a difference."

Chapter 13

THE POLICE VISIT was very short. Dakota arranged for the men to come back the next day to give their statements and potentially to see the jailed prisoner. They could do nothing more tonight.

On the promise of returning the next morning, they headed back to their vehicles. Before too long Saul drove onto a very large property. Foster waited for them outside.

"Wow," she whispered. "I've never seen anything quite so fancy."

"Richard is a doctor and runs a private hospital. He's a really good man."

She nodded. But she didn't say anything else. They went in, and she was escorted to a second-floor bedroom. Saul pushed open the door, turned on the light and said, "Here is your bag you packed."

She stared at in surprise. "So much has happened that I forgot all about this. Hell, I forgot about everything. I should have called Roger at HR and spoken to him."

"It's too late right now."

She nodded. "I have his number. Maybe I'll send him a quick text. He can get back to me in the morning." Pulling out her phone, she sent Roger a message. "There. At least I can sleep better now."

Her phone rang almost immediately. She shot Saul a

surprised look. "It's him."

"Roger?"

"Are you serious about Samantha?" Roger asked. "Oh, my God. What's going on?"

"Yes," she said. "I have to admit, it'll be a long time before I get the picture of her broken body out of my mind."

"With both Tammy and Daniel missing from work, she was working really late in the evenings, making up for the shortfall. We'll figure out exactly what's going on here. And, of course, with you out, that's reason for even more gossip."

"I'm fine. But the others ... I'm not so sure about." She rubbed at the side of her forehead. "Is there anything you can tell me about Samantha's life? I don't even know where she lived."

"I'm sure the cops would be on that."

"I know. The cops will be all over you too," she said, "but I'm working with the private security company that's investigating Daniel's disappearance."

"I don't know what I can tell you about Samantha. That department was tight. At least the men in her department were tight with her. Tammy not so much."

"Yeah, I know that much from Tammy. Daniel's apartment has been cleaned out. Tammy's is untouched, as far as I could see. Mine has been completely annihilated." She quickly explained what they'd found.

"Oh, that's terrible," he said. "Now you're dragged into this mess."

"I just want to find Tammy. I thought I had found her until the flashlights proved it was Samantha."

"Good Lord."

"Where did Samantha come from? What company did she used to work for?"

"Another telecommunication company back East. She was transferred here, and then, within a few months of arriving, she came to us. Look, I can give you her address. I don't think it will help much, and I'm not sure you can get in anyway, not without the police." But he quickly rattled off an address.

"Thanks. I won't tell anyone where I got it from."

"Almost anybody here could've told you. One of our Christmas parties was at her place. You never went or you'd know where she lived too."

"She's not married, doesn't have a family, right?"

"No kids and I don't know if she was living with anyone either. I thought something may have been between her and Daniel. Well, something was between her and Daniel for a little while, but that broke off a year ago."

"Really? I need to know about that." She spoke with him for another few minutes, then hung up.

"Why didn't you go to the Christmas party?" Saul asked.

She shrugged. "Tammy and I had plans to do something together, and the last thing she wanted was to see somebody who she saw enough of at work and didn't like to begin with." Rebel smiled at her surroundings, her focus landing on the freshly made bed. Staring at her clothes, she said, "I need a shower first."

He walked through the room and opened a door. "You have an en suite bath right here." He turned on the light so she could see no one else was around. "My suite is to the right, beside yours." He pointed to the left. "Stone is on the left."

She managed a tired smile. "Now I should sleep the rest of the night."

He walked up to her and dropped a light kiss on her

nose. He started to walk past, stopped, came back. She still stood there, staring at him. He lowered his head and kissed her on the lips. As he lifted his head, he murmured, "Now sleep."

And he walked out.

WALKING OUT WAS one of the hardest things he'd ever done. Yet it was necessary. Even if he wanted to stay and hold her through the night, chances were good neither would get any sleep. And she needed to rest.

He walked to the suite he shared with Dakota.

"Wasn't sure if you would make it back," Dakota joked.

"Of course I was coming back. No chance of it being anything other than that." He tried to keep his voice light instead of letting Dakota know of his turmoil inside.

"But you're interested?"

Saul shrugged. "I'm only here for another day. Like you, I now live in Texas."

"No reason you can't convince her to move back to Texas. Look what Harrison just did."

"Not only Harrison. It's amazing how many women have made the change from the West Coast to Texas."

"Levi should set up a California office. I'm sure we SEAL men can hook up with lots of women who want to *stay* on the West Coast."

Saul shook his head. "I'm enjoying living in Texas. Apparently plenty of women are already in Texas or are happy to move there."

"But you know what? I think, once the heart reaches out, it snags whatever the hell it wants regardless."

"I'm not sure how I feel about her. There is one thing

that I really admire about her."

Dakota said, "Loyalty."

"Okay, so more than one thing." He nodded. "Integrity, honesty and loyalty. They're all the qualities we've cultivated over the last decade. It's the reason we're all happy at Levi's company. That's what we value."

"And that's what all the women who have joined us value too."

Saul walked to the bathroom and took a quick shower. They were short enough on sleep now. And tomorrow could be another busy day. By the time he was done, Dakota was already in the far bed on his laptop. Good, because Saul wanted the bed nearest the door. "What are you looking up?"

"How long it would take you to drive from here to Texas with that Jeep of yours."

"Yeah, I keep going back and forth over that one. I should just sell it."

"Don't do that. You love that thing."

"She's been sitting in California for months now, and it was damn nice to have it again, but I'm not even driving it while I'm here."

"You could."

"Not really. Not if I've got to keep a close eye on Rebel." He got into his bed and turned out the light. "You should get some shut-eye. Morning is coming very damn fast."

Dakota closed his laptop and turned out the last light. "You aren't kidding. Our night is already over."

"Well, I hope tomorrow is a hell of a lot better than today was."

"If you drove the Jeep back, we could send a trailer with her belongings, although she has so little left, you might not need a trailer. She could just buy what she needs in Texas."

"Not happening." Saul refused to even contemplate such a move. Rebel was incredible, but that didn't make her the one for him. At least he didn't think so.

"You know something? I'm not so sure about that." And on that cryptic note, Dakota rolled over and went to sleep.

The trouble was, his words left Saul thinking hard and long before he finally fell asleep himself, taking thoughts of Rebel into his dreams where she made him feel right at home.

Chapter 14

REBEL STARED AT the closed doorway after Saul walked out. She hated to admit it, but, as soon as he left, she felt so alone. The thing was, inside her room she had the privacy to bawl and cry and scream in frustration. But she couldn't find the release to do any of those things. Inside she was just frozen.

Images of Samantha's beaten body tortured her imagination. How could anyone do that to another person? It just wasn't right. It was hard to think of what she might have gone through. Samantha might not have been Rebel's favorite person, but Samantha was still somebody's daughter, mother, sister, sister-in-law, cousin. Someone, somewhere, cared about her.

The fear, the torture and the torment Samantha had gone through was something Rebel wouldn't wish on anybody. The depravity of the human condition was not something she'd been exposed to before this—not to this extent. And she was learning a whole lot she wished she could unlearn. She wasn't sure she could sleep, even though she was exhausted.

The picture of that woman's jaw, her face so damaged, her eye socket bruised and the bloody mess she'd been lying in—this would haunt Rebel's dreams for the rest of her life. If one very small light burned at the end of this, Rebel was thankful the battered body she had found was not Tammy's. But even knowing that, it could still be Tammy lying in a ditch somewhere.

Heartache and grief overwhelmed her. She walked into the bathroom, quickly shedding her clothes. A hot shower would help. Maybe clear her mind and her heart somewhat. Ease the stress in her system.

She caught a glimpse of her face in the bathroom mirror and winced. Somewhere between helping the poor woman and her arrival in this room, she had smeared blood all over her face and the palms of her hands. She stared at the haggard woman looking back at her and realized just how much this week had taken from her.

She turned away resolutely. There would be no quitting until she found Tammy. Unmindful of the time, she stepped under the hot water and let the heat pound on her back, her head and her shoulders. When she turned her face into the rainlike downpour, she wasn't sure where the shower started and her tears stopped. Or how long she stood there, letting her emotions ripple through her system.

Finally, wrapped up in a towel, she walked toward the bed and gave her hair a quick towel-dry, then pulled out a T-shirt and panties to wear as she crawled into bed.

Her head barely hit the pillow, and she was tossed into a nightmare that screamed with rage and pain.

She woke less than an hour later, covered in sweat, her body shaking, panic coursing through her. She kicked off the blankets and lay trembling as the cool morning air dried off her sweat-soaked skin. She shuddered.

Her life had become this never-ending nightmare. She didn't know how to get out of it.

As she lay wondering if it would be okay to search for

the kitchen and get a glass of herbal tea, sirens ripped through the house. She bolted to her feet and froze. It wasn't a fire alarm. The raging drive of an odd pitch had her slapping her hands over her ears. Footsteps raced outside in the hallway. She ran toward the door as Saul opened it from the other side.

"An intruder is on the property."

She stared at him, her mouth dropping. "Holy crap, that's the security alarm?"

He nodded.

She put on her bathrobe, slipping her arms through the sleeves, and returned to the hallway with him.

"Do you want to stay here?" he asked, searching her face.

She shook her head. "No, I'll stay where you are. No way do I want to be separated from you guys."

He nodded and led the way into the kitchen.

She glanced around at the empty place. "Where has everybody gone?"

"Foster's in the security room, checking out the video cameras. He will have sent everyone off in different directions."

"Then we should be there to show we are fine?"

He gave her a lopsided smile. "I'm here to keep you safe."

She rolled her eyes. "That means you're on babysitting duty. I can be in the security room with Foster just as easily as anywhere else."

He seemed to consider that, then nodded. "Come this way then."

He led her through several halls and up a short set of stairs into another room.

By the time they walked through the doorway she was

completely lost as to how they got here. "This place is a maze. Nobody would ever find their way here."

Foster glanced up and smiled at her. "I'm so sorry for disturbing your sleep," he apologized.

She smiled at the older man. "I'd just woken up from a horrible nightmare, so this is a grateful reprieve. I hope whoever it is has not caused any real damage."

"He'll have to get to that point first," Foster said cheerfully. "And I'll make sure he doesn't."

She smiled. "I'll just sit here. You all have something useful to do, I assume."

Beside her, Saul muttered, "Keeping you alive and well is useful."

She shot him a look. "I'm fine. Go do your hero stuff."

At that term Foster chuckled. Saul glared at her.

She stared at him in surprise. "What did I say?"

"Nothing," he muttered. He shot Foster a hard look. "Right, Foster?" But Foster was laughing too hard.

She shrugged. "I'm glad you guys are having fun with this, but what about the intruder?"

Saul reached out and tapped the monitor. "There he is."

Sure enough, a black-dressed figure slid alongside the guesthouse.

"Don't even know where that building is," she said.

"It's my house," Foster said with a note of outrage.

"Oh, dear," she said. "That doesn't sound very good."

But the intruder slid past Foster's house and raced across the distance toward the main house. While she watched, a second man stepped in, his arm straight out, connecting with the intruder's throat. And just like that the intruder went down.

"Oh, my God! Is that one of our guys?" Then she recognized the shape and snorted. "Of course that's Stone. No way it isn't him." Inside she was elated. Not only had the response time been very short, but they had caught the intruder. Then another thought crossed her mind. "Do you think there's a second man?"

Saul said, "Almost certainly. No reason for them to come alone on a mission like this. I'm presuming you know why they're coming?"

She shook her head.

"The only thing that's changed is you. They're here for you."

She stared at him in horror. "But I'm nobody."

"Apparently you're somebody who had the USB key. You're the one who's been the driving force behind the search for Tammy."

She shook her head. "That is not good. I didn't want anything to do with any of this."

She sat back in her seat a little dumbfounded, considering that any of this revolved around her. "The focus should be on Tammy," she announced. "This has nothing to do with me."

"And what if there was more information than what was on the USB key, and they think you might either have a copy of it or a second key?"

She shook her head. "Hell no. I didn't know anything about that first key, so how could I know anything about a second one?"

Foster turned to look at her. "Any chance two different parties are involved in this? And the key went to one while the other party either doesn't know that or thinks you might've kept a copy of it?"

Her jaw dropped. "This is getting way too convoluted.

Why would a second party be in this?"

"What if somebody was selling information to the highest bidder?" Saul asked. "That could involve many interested parties."

Saul's words cut through her heart. "If anybody did that, it would have been Samantha. Tammy would have nothing to do with this. And I mean, *nothing*."

The men nodded. "We hear you. That doesn't make it so. Something's going on, and it's tough because we don't have the right people to talk to. We need Daniel and Tammy."

At that, Rebel saw movement out of the corner of her eye. Gasping, she pointed. "Look!"

Sure enough, a second man dressed in black was in the kitchen. She bounded to her feet. "He's inside the house," she cried out.

"Keep her here." Saul slipped outside the security room.

She didn't know where Dakota or Merk were or if anybody could communicate with them. Saul shouldn't be handling this guy on his own. She headed to the door behind him.

Foster's voice cut through the small room. "He'll handle it just fine on his own."

"What if that guy's not alone? What if there's more than one man in the kitchen?"

Foster leaned forward to study the monitors. "At the moment, there is just one man."

"Can you tell if the others are nearby?"

He pointed to different monitors, showing her. Stone and Merk stood over the first man, still unconscious. Stone reached down and grabbed one arm; Merk grabbed the other, and they hauled him toward the house.

"Where's Dakota?"

"He's on the far side of the property."

"So that leaves Saul all alone."

He glanced at her. "Saul will be just fine."

She bit her lower lip. "I have self-defense training."

"But are you very good against bullets?" He tapped the monitor for her to see the intruder had a gun.

"Oh, my God!" She bolted for the door, opened it and raced after Saul. She tried to retrace his steps, but she faced multiple hallways and different stairs. By the time she made her way to the kitchen, it was empty.

And she knew she'd done something wrong. And so very foolish. Under her breath she swore, "Shit."

But, knowing where the cameras were so Foster could keep an eye on her, she walked into the kitchen and proceeded to put on coffee. She figured such a mundane task could bring the intruder to her, and Saul could go after them or anybody watching her.

The problem was, her hands were shaking. When she finally turned on the coffee, she pivoted and leaned against the counter.

Only to see a man dressed in black with a gun pointed at her head.

She sucked in her breath. And stared at him. This was not how she had planned her morning.

SAUL SLIPPED INTO the dining room as the man headed to the kitchen. Saul decided to go around. Heading back the way he'd come, he took a different direction and came up on the far end of the dining room. He heard the sound of light footsteps. Steps that could only belong to Rebel.

She was supposed to stay with Foster. What the hell was she doing down here? Just as suddenly he heard motion in the kitchen, and he shook his head. *Coffee.* He crept closer, knowing the sounds that attracted him would definitely attract the intruder.

"There you are, bitch."

The words seemed to hit his heart. He snuck over to the side entrance to see the man standing with a gun trained on Rebel. Her white-knuckled grip showed the tension she otherwise refused to let the gunman see.

"What the hell do you want?" she asked. "This is not your home. You're trespassing. We handed over the USB key, and we were supposed to get Tammy and Daniel back."

"Which they couldn't do because they don't have them."

Saul watched her straighten in disbelief.

"As I have them."

"Why should I believe you?"

"I don't give a shit if you do or not."

"Where are Tammy and Daniel?" she demanded.

"I have them."

"Did you torture them like that other asshole did to Samantha?" Her glare was direct, and, as much as Saul wished she would not dive face-first into trouble, he had to admire her courage and tenacity.

"No. But Samantha deserves what she gets. She sold the data she stole from Daniel, but someone else got wind of the deal. They hired me to act as a go-between and convince her to sell it to me instead. So she's a thief and a double-crosser."

"But why? Why did the first buyer want the information, and why would you care?"

"According to Samantha, the other buyer was looking for blackmail material to gain concessions. Whereas the company I'm selling to is looking to crash the market share, pressuring your company into a takeover at a much cheaper price."

"And how does Tammy fit into this?"

"Damn bitch figured out what was happening, so she took a copy of the information and proof of Samantha's involvement to turn over to the head of the company."

"She should've taken it to the police."

The man shrugged. "Doesn't matter what she should've done. She can't do anything about it now."

"So what do you want from me?"

"I need a copy of Tammy's information. Otherwise I can't get my fee."

Rebel stared at him and shook her head. "The only key I found was turned over to the other guy to get Tammy back. And we got Samantha back for that. But now you need a copy from me to get Tammy and Daniel back?" She held out her hands and spread them wide. "Where the hell do you expect me to find a copy of that information? If it even exists, which I doubt."

"It exists. These IT people, they never make a single copy. They always make a backup copy. And I want that copy."

"Is it worth killing over?"

"I didn't kill anyone."

Saul watched the relief wash over Rebel's face. "Is Tammy still alive?"

He nodded. "Still, this won't end well if I don't get that backup copy and fast."

She shook her head. "I'm not interested in doing any deals until I get Tammy back. I already paid the initial price, and all I got was a dead IT supervisor."

"What do you mean, *dead?*"

Saul watched as Rebel nodded slowly.

"Samantha was alive when I found her. But she died in minutes. That asshole who beat her to death was also responsible for killing a homeless man, then shot two of his own men."

"Very interesting." The intruder thought about that for a moment, then shrugged. "I guess everybody has a price."

Suddenly the gunman stepped back into the shadows. Saul slipped farther back.

"Tell me who is out there." The gunman shifted his gun and said, "Now."

She sighed and said, "I don't know who's out there."

Saul walked into the kitchen casually.

When she stared at him in shock, he just shrugged.

The gunman turned, the gun now pointed at the two of them. "Where's a copy of the material you handed over?"

"On my laptop," Saul said.

"I need a copy."

Saul tilted his head, his gaze locked on the intruder's eyes. "I can do that. But I need my laptop and something to copy the data to."

The gunman fished into his pocket and pulled out a USB key. "Put it on this."

Saul shook his head. "I'm not doing anything with a gun held on her."

The gun shifted to him.

Saul turned to Rebel and said, "Get my laptop. It's on my bed, honey."

She opened her mouth to protest when the gun shifted her way, and the guy in black said, "Do it now or I'll shoot him."

"I thought you weren't into killing?" She glared at the gunman, making Saul grin.

"As there are already dead bodies, I can make it look like it's not my doing."

She gave a shuttered look, turned and walked from the kitchen.

Saul smiled when he saw no victim stance in her spine. She was pissed.

She went upstairs, and, within a few minutes, she came back down, carrying the laptop. She put it on the kitchen table, opened it and turned it on, then stepped back.

Saul walked over, put in the USB key, quickly accessed the information Merk had emailed out as a copy to everyone and copied it over. When he was done, he pulled out the key and handed it to the gunman.

Just as it was supposed to cross hands, she stepped forward. "No, wait."

Saul turned to look at her.

"Not without getting Tammy first."

The gunman cocked the gun and held it against Saul's head. "I give the orders."

She glared at him. "And I've been cheated. You give the orders right now to release both of them, and I want them back here."

"Or I just shoot both of you, grab the information and run."

"What makes you think you'll be able to run?" she taunted. "You get nothing if I don't get everything. We need two hostages back—you want the information. It's a simple trade. You must have somebody watching over them. You get them delivered right now to the front gates here. We'll walk you out. You get the key. We get our people."

He glared at her in frustration. "I'm the one with the gun, so, you see, that gives me the upper hand."

She snatched the key from Saul's hand. "And now I have the USB key, so if you're planning on shooting both of us right now, do it fast before I kick the bones in your nose through your brain. Or you can make a deal."

He stared at her in frustration. "You don't understand how this works, bitch."

She gave a feral smile. "No, I didn't learn how to play terrorism well. I failed kidnapping class too. But I can tell you one thing, I passed martial arts. And I will push your brain out the back your head and use your nose to do it. So tell me right now if you're up for this deal."

Her tone was so damn fierce that Saul almost didn't recognize it.

"Pull out your goddamn phone and make the call." When he didn't move, she snapped, "Now!"

"You really think you can kick me faster that I can shoot you?"

"I can't guarantee that bullet won't stop me." She wasn't alone as Saul had some pretty fine skills himself. "What I can guarantee is that"—she made slow steps, widening the gap between her and Saul—"between the two of us, you will never walk out of this house."

He pulled out his phone and made a quick call to leave the two hostages at the front of 427 Remington Park. "I'll meet you out front." Then he turned to her. "Done."

She nodded. "I hope that was a real call you made. Because I'm doing the countdown on your life now."

Saul wished he could reach out and gently hold her hand, but the distance between them prevented that. Instead he spoke softly to her. "It'll be okay. Just take it easy."

The gunman snorted. "You are totally nuts to have her in your life. How can you ever trust she won't kill you?"

Rebel laughed.

Saul smiled. "I trust her just fine."

The gunman shrugged. "Your funeral. You make sure everyone else stays away. I don't know who else is here, but let's make this simple, no bloodshed. You guys brought it to this point."

"*We* did this?" Rebel growled. "No, you and the other greedy selfish cowardly asshole, hiding behind guns and threats, *did this*." Then she laughed, like a loon.

Even with a ski mask on, the gunman couldn't hide the fear in his eyes.

Saul was pretty sure that was Rebel's game plan.

Abruptly she stopped, mid-laugh. "But we'll finish this for sure."

The gunman stepped back, waving the gun between her, then Saul, then at her again.

"Our guns have been trained on you from the moment you entered this kitchen," Saul said.

At his words Dakota, Merk and Stone all stepped inside the kitchen.

The intruder took one look at the guns trained on him, then glared down at Rebel and snapped, "So that's where your bravado came from." He slowly lowered his gun.

She shoved her face into his. "Like hell it was."

The gunman stepped back and glanced at Saul. "She's one crazy bitch. If you are willing to take a walk on the wild side, that's your problem, buddy. But I prefer to wake up in the morning and smile at my woman, not check to see if she's ready to kill me."

"I would never worry about something like that with

her." Saul wrapped his arm around Rebel's shoulders, tucked firmly against his side, so she wouldn't charge into the middle of the play going on. There was a time to be fiery and a time to be moderate. Right now things were shifting quickly. Being in the middle of a gunfight was not a position he'd like to see her in. With everyone else now surrounding the gunman, the roles had changed.

"You need to let me go," the gunman said.

The gun hung uselessly from his fingers. Nobody made a move to step forward and take it.

"Why is that?" Merk asked from behind him.

"Because otherwise your friends won't make it. They might make it to the gate, but, if I'm not there, they won't drop them off."

"That's easy. We'll move you to the gate for them," Dakota said. "We won't forget how you came into a friend of ours house with a gun, waving it around, making demands, uttering threats. Plus you've kidnapped two of our friends, which is not only an act of war but something we'll not forgive easily. Now you're here acting as if you're the boss?"

The gunman shot a look at Dakota and snorted. "He who has the gun is the boss."

"Guns are not the be-all and end-all," Rebel snapped. "And right now a lot of *bosses* are in this kitchen, and you're not one of them."

He shot her a look of utter dislike. "You need to watch your mouth."

"And you need to watch for my foot to connect with your nose."

He dropped back as if she had made physical contact.

She smiled, shoved her chin upward. For some reason

Saul found it incredibly cute. He tugged her closer and dropped a kiss on her temple. She turned and shot him a look of complete shock.

He chuckled. "I couldn't resist."

She shook her head and muttered, "You're nuts."

The gunman shook his head. "He's a complete whack job if he's interested in you."

She turned to glare at him, but Saul kept her tight against him. "I suggest we take this party outside. I would not appreciate anybody shooting up Richard's house."

"We also need to get the hostages, if there's any chance of them coming," Rebel said with emphasis.

Stone stepped forward and nudged the gunman. At the same time he pulled the gun free from the man's fingers. "Outside," he snapped.

The gunman walked silently forward. So many men had guns trained on him that he'd be a fool to try anything.

But Saul didn't trust him. Saul hadn't gotten this far in life without having a few tricks up his sleeve. What he didn't know was if anymore gunmen were outside. The men exchanged hard glances.

They split up, two of them leading the gunman out to the gate.

Foster, as if understanding what was going on, opened the gate from the control room.

Saul wished he could send Rebel back to Foster but knew she would never allow that to happen. He kept the farthest back, hanging tightly to the wild card named Rebel, keeping an eye on everything going on around him, his gaze searching for hidden threats. He slowly led her forward. She tried to break free of his arm, but he clenched his arm tighter around her shoulders and said, "Wait. We don't know if he's alone."

She froze. Her gaze darted in all directions.

"We'll get there. It's all about timing now. I don't want him to hit the gate before the vehicle arrives with the hostages."

She nodded. "Okay."

But he didn't ease up his grip. She was too impulsive to understand how sensitive this exchange was. Anything could go wrong, and then the five of them would be dead, and the gunman would be laughing his head off. That was not the way this would go down.

As Stone and Merk pushed the gunman forward, a vehicle drove down the long driveway. It was fronted by a private road and then veered off on to become this long drive up to the gated residence. As the vehicle came closer, Merk stepped off to one side and disappeared into the shadows. Stone stood right beside the gunman, his weapon out of sight.

The vehicle opened up. Two men got out. They opened the back doors and dragged out two people. Hearing Rebel's gasp beside him, Saul clapped a hand over her mouth. "Hush."

She nodded frantically, but she still tried to wiggle free of his grasp. He wouldn't let go. It was damn hard to hold her back though.

In a harsh whisper he said, "No."

She stilled and shot him a look of dislike. He grinned. But he refused to let up. The hostages hit the ground, both unconscious. The gunman took a step forward, speaking to his men. "We're leaving now."

"What about your buddy?" she asked bitterly. "I guess you're okay to leave a man behind."

He ignored her, walking over to the vehicle, USB key in hand. He slid into the back seat; they got into the front of the vehicle and drove off.

Chapter 15

"WHY DIDN'T WE confirm that was Tammy and Daniel first? Why didn't we stop them from leaving?" Rebel cried out. She raced forward to see the victims on the ground. The first was Daniel and the second, yes, Tammy. She dropped to her friend's side and quickly untied the gag around her mouth. She checked the unconscious woman for a pulse. "She's still alive. We need an ambulance."

Just as the words escaped her mouth, she heard shooting. She bolted to her feet and saw some kind of confrontation at the far end of the driveway. "What's going on?"

"The police. They were waiting down below for the kidnapper's vehicle. They had orders to let them come in but to stop them on their way out."

She turned to stare at Saul. "Who told them to do that?"

"I did," Foster said from the sidelines with dignity. He walked up and stood beside Daniel, gave him a once-over medically and then went to Tammy. "Nobody walks into my house with a gun unless I say so."

"Your house?" Rebel asked.

"Richard is my employer, and this house is my responsibility." His tone said he was almost insulted.

"I'm sorry," Rebel said. "I didn't mean to insult you."

"I've been looking after Richard for a very long time.

And that extends to his property." After a quick exam of Tammy, he said, "She appears to be drugged."

Rebel stared down at her friend, seeing the chafe marks from being tied up and the dried blood on her fingers along with bruising on her arms and face. She held Tammy's hand against her chest and whispered, "Tammy, wake up, please. Tammy, wake up." But there were no conscious signs of life, although her chest rose and fell on a steady basis. "I guess by keeping them drugged they didn't have to worry about them causing any trouble."

"Exactly."

Tammy's clothes were definitely dirty, torn and blood-stained, but she didn't appear to have sustained any of the physical violence that Samantha had. And, for that, Rebel was grateful. In the distance she could hear the sound of sirens from emergency vehicles. She waited anxiously for the ambulance to pull up. When it did, two EMTs hopped out; one raced over to the victims while the other one pulled out a gurney.

Saul and Dakota walked to the ambulance, pulled out the second gurney, bringing it over. Carefully Daniel was loaded in the ambulance and then Tammy.

Rebel climbed into the back of the ambulance beside Tammy. She looked at Saul, standing at the doorway. "I don't have my purse."

He motioned for her to come back out. "We'll get you dressed and follow the ambulance to the hospital."

That's when she realized she wore her oversized T-shirt, panties and a bathrobe, exposing her bare legs, yet she wasn't cold. "Oh, dear Lord." She accepted his help back out of the ambulance and stood in the circle of his arms as the vehicle took off with its precious cargo. She hadn't realized, while the ambulance had been here, two cop cars had joined the fray. When she saw the first policeman, she cried out, "Did you catch that vehicle and the gunmen?"

He nodded. "Driver and passengers. Three men rounded up and taken into custody. They aren't very happy."

Foster stepped up and said, "I have plenty of videotape evidence showing the intruders trespassing on private property, one coming into the main house, threatening my guests with a gun and the vehicle they called to collect him, dropping off the two unconscious hostages who have just been taken away."

The policeman nodded. "Now that is good news. We would like copies of all those tapes please."

Foster, wrapped in a housecoat, nodded. "I can do that now." He turned to one of the policemen. "Come with me."

The two men walked inside, and Rebel saw that, even in moments of crisis, Foster remained dignified and calm. He'd done better than she had. It was such a relief to know they had Tammy, and the criminals had been caught.

And now that all the excitement was over, she realized she was cold, tired and struggling to stay on her feet. The guys had been right—she had to look after herself to be able to help Tammy. Now that her friend was safe, maybe Rebel could grab a couple hours for herself.

"Saul, can I go back to bed?"

He glanced at her in surprise. "You can sleep?"

She shook her head. "I don't know, but I'm exhausted, like all the adrenaline left my body at once," she admitted. "I don't want to be here. I want to be with Tammy. But you're right. She's unconscious, and I'm a mess. If I can grab a couple hours, by then the doctors would have checked her over, and maybe I can be with her. I'm not family … so …"

"Go," Saul, said motioning to the house behind him.

"I'll be fine," she said, then motioned to the cops. "You have plenty to deal with here."

"So do you," he said quietly. "You have to give a statement to the police as well."

She winced. "Maybe I should do that first." But she really wanted to sleep. "I don't have anything to add to what you guys say."

Just then one of the cops walked over. He had more than a few questions. Understanding that she should corroborate their statements to make this clean and simple, she answered as fast as she could. When she started to run down, she said, "If you don't mind, I need to lay down." She wrapped her arms around her chest. "And I'm beyond chilled."

The police officer nodded and took down her contact information.

"You might as well talk to Detective Wilson. He's already got everything. He's the one I've been talking to about Tammy's disappearance."

"Well, it's nice to know you didn't give up on her."

She gave him a misty smile. "Tammy's a good friend of mine. I don't leave anybody I love behind."

With a smile at Saul she turned and walked back inside. To say she was chilled was an understatement. She was beyond cold now. She bowed her head against the cool morning air and stepped inside.

Foster was there to greet everyone, pouring coffee. He looked at her sharply. "Do you want coffee first or a hot shower?"

Her teeth started to chatter. "I'd say both," she whispered, "but I couldn't drink it—or safely carry it—anyway.

I'll have a hot shower and crawl into bed, if I can."

He nodded and watched as she escaped. Upstairs she really wanted to bypass the shower and curl up in bed. For whatever reason she wanted to bawl her eyes out too. Tammy had been found, but Rebel's relief was lost in waves of emotions—which made absolutely no sense.

She tossed the few clothes she had on to the bathroom floor and stepped under the hot shower water. Instantly a heated cloud filled the room. She was desperate to get warm, but the chill seemed to be inside her. And that just told her how wrong everything was. There was no reason for this now. Tammy was in the hospital—she didn't appear to be horrifically injured. Although she had been drugged, and that was definitely a concern, Rebel had every hope her friend would recover.

She'd done it. She'd found her friend. She should be laughing, cheering. Not bawling.

But still she didn't know what her friend had been through over eleven long days. She didn't know what drug Tammy had been given, in what dosages, for how long; and Rebel would in no way feel reassured until she had a chance to speak with her friend. Saul was right; it would take a while for the hospital staff to assess what those assholes had done to Tammy. And Rebel wasn't family, so she probably couldn't stay at her best friend's bedside.

After standing under the hot water as long as she felt she could, she stepped from the shower, wrapping a towel around her. The outside of her had warmed up, but her insides hadn't. She exchanged the damp towel for her bathrobe, quickly towel-drying her hair of excess water and tossing the towel to the tile floor, and then made her way to the bed. Still wrapped up in the bathrobe, she tucked under the bedcovers.

Just as she got settled, a knock came at her door.

"Come in." And damn if her teeth hadn't started to chatter again.

Saul stuck his head around the door. His gaze zeroed in on her face with concern. "You don't look so good." He stepped inside, bringing her a hot cup of coffee.

She shivered. "I had a hot shower. I don't know why I'm still shivering so much."

"Shock," he said. "You've been through an unbelievable eleven days. Now that we found your friend, your body is in protest."

She shuddered and huddled deeper into the blankets. He set down the cup of coffee, walked around to the far side of the bed and lay down on top, pulling her against him. He just held her. "Just remember, she's okay now. We found her, and, thanks to you, she wasn't allowed to be forgotten."

"But I was so close to not finding her," she whispered. "I'll have nightmares about what ..."

"I know how that feels," he admitted. "But you can only do so much. You have to remember, we found her. As soon as she wakes up from the drugs, and the doctors have a chance to check her over, then you can see her. No point in you sitting in the hospital, suffering physically and emotionally yourself, when you can't be at her side."

"I understand that, which is why I'm here in bed. But I can't seem to get warm."

He pulled her firmly against him and wrapped himself around her. "Give it a minute. The heat should kick in soon. If you want some coffee, it'll help warm up the inside pretty fast. Foster put some whiskey in it for you."

She made a garbled laugh. "I can't stand whiskey at the

best of times."

"I think it's for medicinal purposes, not for enjoyment."

"In that case …"

He helped her sit up slightly and gave her the coffee. It was just about drinking temperature. She took several deep gulps and winced. "It still tastes disgusting." He replaced the cup on the bedside table, and she curled up in bed once again. He wrapped his arms around her.

If nothing else it did make her feel a hell of a lot better. "Do you think she'll be okay?"

"According to the paramedics they can't see any reason for her not to make a full recovery, but we don't know what kind of drugs were used. And that'll make all the difference in her recovery time."

"I'm so scared that, after all she's been through, she still won't make it."

"Remember to have hope. We found her against slim odds just hours ago."

She nodded. "Just so damn scary."

"Rest, curl up, stay warm and sleep."

Slowly the trembling stopped, and she breathed easier. At the same time her thoughts drifted in and out. As he shifted and tried to withdraw, she grabbed his hand and held him close. "Please stay."

He settled back on the bed beside her and tucked her against his chest. "Sleep. I won't go anywhere."

She pulled her head back enough to look into his eyes.

He smiled, dropped a kiss on her nose and said, "I promise."

And she knew she could trust him. There was just something about these men. They were all good, honorable men. They wouldn't have left anybody behind. Even now.

She closed her eyes and slept.

SAUL RELAXED AND held Rebel close. She was well-named. She was such a mix of feistiness and loyalty, with a bit of nervous kitten thrown in, that he knew he'd need a long time getting to truly understand who she was on the inside. He really wanted that chance.

Shitty timing on his move to Texas. Although he might ask for every job that California offered, he would spend the bulk of every year away from her. And that was no way to build a relationship. It was one of the reasons why he'd stayed away from building permanent attachments when he was in the military. They were damn hard. He never married, never got close to the altar. He watched all his friends' relationships fall apart throughout the years, his buddies falling to pieces when their marriages broke up and they lost track of their kids or split the beds between them. He vowed to never do that. It wasn't the way he wanted his life to go.

Then he had left the military and joined Levi's group. And that showed him a whole different level of stable loving relationships he couldn't have imagined before. But that didn't mean he was ready for one. Then again, like in Harrison's case, love had just hit Harrison upside the head. Had that just happened to Saul?

He gently stroked Rebel's arm as she slept against his chest. This was not what he'd expected when he'd arrived in California.

He heard a soft tap on the door. The knob turned, and Dakota poked his head around the corner. "There you are."

"She couldn't sleep."

Dakota nodded. "We're having a meeting in the kitchen. I'll tell the guys you'll be down in a bit."

Saul nodded. "Give me a couple minutes to make sure she's under. She needs sleep first and foremost."

Dakota nodded and slowly withdrew.

Saul lay there, knowing he was enjoying stolen moments. He didn't know if there'd be a next time to lie here and just hold her close. She was very special. At the same time, he had a responsibility to the men downstairs. They had an awful mess to clean up. They had come to find Daniel, had done so. For all Saul knew, he would get pulled away and sent back to Texas. And this moment would be over. Maybe never to happen again. He winced at that thought.

She murmured against his neck. "Saul?"

He gently reached out and brushed her cheek. "Yes, it's me."

A gentle sigh whispered from her lips, and she sank back down into sleep. He waited a few moments to see how deeply she slept, and then he shifted ever-so-slightly as if to roll away from her. She murmured a protest but rolled over to the other side and curled up in a ball.

Hating to do it, but knowing it was the right thing to do, he slipped off the bed. With one last glance at her, he slowly withdrew from the room and closed the door lightly behind him. He made his way to the kitchen.

The guys all hung around the table. He walked over to the coffee pot, poured himself a cup and joined them.

"How is she?" Foster asked. "She came in just trembling."

Saul nodded. "She's pretty shaken up. She's asleep finally. I think the shock is evidence of what she's been through in the last eleven days. The reality just hit her."

"And yet, we found Tammy," Dakota said.

"And she's racked with the *what ifs* right now."

Understanding crossed everyone's face. They all knew what that meant.

Every one of them had been in cases where it had been damn close, where they had been so afraid that, if they hadn't done just one little thing, there would've been a different outcome—a much worse one. By the same token, they'd all been in circumstances where they couldn't do the one little thing that could save somebody. And they'd all lost somebody. The *what ifs* were the stuff of nightmares.

"When she wakes up, I presume she'll go to the hospital?" Merk asked. "We have an update. Daniel and Tammy are still under observation. Both had been heavily sedated—not sure what drugs were used yet. We do know they aren't sporting broken bones, and neither have been beaten like Samantha was."

"Different kidnappers presumably," Saul said. He took a sip of coffee and sat down. A night without sleep wasn't unheard of for any of them. But he was feeling it himself. Nothing he'd like better than to go upstairs and lie down for a few hours.

With a look at his watch, he realized it was only four o'clock in the morning, and nothing could be done for a while. They made a quick list of what they'd have to do, and then they split up for two hours.

Saul walked upstairs to his bedroom, stripped down to his boxers and lay down on his bed. Two hours sleep wasn't much, but he knew from past experience it was often all he'd get.

As he lay there with his eyes closed, he heard a whimper.

He realized it was Rebel, once again suffering in her dreams. He got up, walked out to the hall and stepped into her room. She was curled up in a tight ball in the bed, the tears pouring down her cheeks. He slipped under the covers, wrapped his arms around her and pulled her tight against him. She relaxed and fell into a deep sleep. He smiled. Now he could sleep too.

He drifted in and out, waking every once in a while as she surfaced, stroking her arm or back or her cheek, calming her down again until she slept.

He woke in the morning light to see her sitting up in bed, staring down at him. He smiled. "How do you feel?"

"Considering we slept together, I feel fine."

That startled a laugh out of him. "Weren't you expecting to feel fine if we slept together?"

She smirked. "I expected to feel great, in that case."

"Well, the only excuse I can give you is I've been here less than two hours." He glanced at his watch and groaned. "We're supposed to be meeting in the kitchen at seven for breakfast, and then we start the day, and it'll be a full one."

She nodded. "Are you leaving now that you've found Daniel?"

"Yes. We're meeting a few men in the morning then flying out."

She winced. "That's too bad." She studied him for a long moment. "I'd like to spend more time with you."

"Ditto."

"So how long do we have?" she asked with a wicked grin.

Saul stared at her in surprise. "For what?"

She stroked the side of his face. "Don't be dense." And she tugged him toward her. "You've given me several kisses," she whispered. "But you did not kiss me properly yet." And she pulled him the rest of the way down, planting a searing, passionate, wet kiss on him, sending his blood pressure soaring.

He hadn't expected this, but, with his training, he was prepared for anything. He slipped his hands underneath her body, up to her long hair. His fingers slid against her scalp, tugging her head back as he shifted on top of her—placing his instant erection right where he wanted it to be.

She chuckled. "Glad to see you're up for the job."

He grinned. "Absolutely." And he kissed her with hot, passionate, needy kisses that neither could deny. There was no prelude to this. There was no foreplay. This was an instant need. This was heat striking through their systems, lightning passing through, burning through their insides as lips and hands demanded more.

She lifted her hips against him and whispered, "Now."

He pulled back, gasping for air. "Not yet."

She leaned forward and nipped him on the shoulder. "Yes."

He groaned. "Not so fast. I want to make this last."

"Next time. We'll make it last next time."

She flipped him to his back and straddled him. She quickly pulled off the bathrobe she'd worn to bed, leaving her bare in the early morning light then his boxers were slid off his hips and flung to the floor. His hand stroked upward to cup her plump breasts as he watched this Amazon woman slide forward and brace her arms beside his chest before lowering herself onto his shaft.

Then he couldn't think at all. She rode him hard and then harder—fast and then faster—until he gripped her hips and pounded into her.

She cried out, her body arching backward until her hips

stilled.

"No," he groaned and he lifted hard and heavy, grinding into her heat, shooting up one more time to pierce as deep as he could before his own climax ripped through him.

She shuddered and collapsed on top of him. He sagged in exhaustion, his breath raspy and hard. "Damn, woman. You want to kill me?"

She chuckled. "Not yet, but maybe in an hour."

He glanced at his watch and realized they had about half that, maybe a little longer.

She propped her forearms on his chest and smiled down at him. "Ready for round two?"

He rolled his eyes, but there was no stopping her. She slid down him, her lips and hands busy, enticing, tangling, stroking, caressing, pinching as she explored his body at will. He groaned, holding her in place, but she wasn't having any of it.

She whispered, "We don't have enough time. I want a night with you."

"I want weeks with you," he whispered. "Maybe even a lifetime."

But she was wiggling and moving, sliding, kissing him, her hands everywhere, making it hard to stop their tormenting journey. His body was alive with nerve endings as she stroked and caressed, cupped and squeezed.

When he couldn't take it anymore, he grabbed her, slammed her to the bed underneath him and entered her in one thrust.

She stilled, smiled up at him, wrapped her thighs around his hips and said, "Now."

And he drove them both to the finish line. A good ten minutes later he lifted his head and collapsed to the side. She made a murmured protest, which he ignored. "I can't believe I have to get up and face them now."

She couldn't help teasing him. "I don't have to. I can get up and have a shower."

"That's not fair," he protested.

They sat up and looked at the clock, realizing he was late. He leaned over, gave her a hard kiss and said, "I have to get dressed, and my clothes are in my room."

She chuckled. "Make sure nobody sees you."

He rolled his eyes. He opened the door, snuck from her room and, just as he crept into his suite, a creak sounded on the stairway. He turned to see Dakota standing there with a big grin on his face. Saul rolled his eyes, stepped inside and slammed the door a little too hard. Dakota's laughter rolled down the hall. Damn if Saul couldn't hear Rebel's chuckles too. He got in a quick shower and a shave and then dressed. By that time he was grinning like a fool.

Life was damn fine.

Chapter 16

REBEL SAT BESIDE the hospital bed. Tammy had been moved from Intensive Care into a regular room. She had come out of the drug-induced stupor and was now sleeping naturally. The doctors warned it would take at least a day—if not two—for the charcoal treatment to extract the drugs fully from her system. That was good news for Rebel. The last thing she wanted was to think Tammy needed weeks to recover from her ordeal.

Rebel knew psychologically it would take a lot longer, and that Tammy would need counseling of some kind to deal with the trauma of what she'd been through. Daniel was in a similar position, although he'd taken a bit more of a beating. He looked like he had resisted in some way, as he had a couple broken ribs. Rebel hadn't been in to see him yet. She kept hoping Tammy would wake up, and Rebel wanted to be sitting beside her best friend when she did.

Knowing Tammy would eventually be fine, Rebel settled back in her chair and waited. She'd had almost no sleep last night, and just to know that she could relax now was huge. She wished she had brought her laptop with her so she would have something to do.

Her life had been on hold for eleven days. Even now she wasn't sure what had happened to her job. Did she have one still? She had phoned her boss, left a message. But nobody got back to her. She'd walked out, taking her week's holiday, but then should have returned a few days ago, only she hadn't gone back yet. But she did touch base with her boss earlier, giving him the update on Samantha. Still, that was not the way to keep her job. At the same time, her apartment had been gutted. Now that things had calmed, she should properly notify her landlord. Those crime scene tapes on her door weren't the first way he would want to find out. Because those repairs would take time, she needed a place to live until then. She also had to notify her insurance company of the loss she had sustained.

She just didn't know what to do. She was torn because she knew Saul was a large part of her indecision. She hadn't expected to find anybody in this crazy world, but she had. She didn't want to see him go, even while she sat beside Tammy.

But Saul would be sent back to Texas soon. And Rebel couldn't leave Tammy in San Diego.

Even though he had lived in California, his life was in Texas now. She was at a crossroads, but she had probably lost her job and had no place to go. She also had no real reason to go to Texas either—except for him.

She sniffled. If she'd met him when he still lived in California, maybe she could have convinced him to stay. Then she thought about what she'd been through for the last week and a half. Some things in life she couldn't go back to.

She thought about asking for and returning to her job, but everything inside of her revolted. She hadn't been kidnapped, and she hadn't gone through any of that subsequent abuse, but several people she worked with had. She was emotionally affected.

Inasmuch as she enjoyed her job, she certainly didn't

want to work with that same group who had done this to Tammy and Daniel. And Samantha.

Nothing would replace the ugly memories of the last eleven days. And it would take her a long time to stop seeing Samantha's battered face and broken body.

Rebel knew the police would be looking into her employer in a big way, and she didn't want to be a part of that either. Once her name was linked to the investigation, especially since she had handed over the damning information that would damage her company's reputation—twice—she for damn sure didn't have a job to go back to, based on that alone.

She groaned, picked up her feet, set them gently on the edge of Tammy's bed and leaned back, closing her eyes.

What a mess.

"Rebel?"

Rebel bolted to her feet and stared down at Tammy, whose eyes were open, a little cloudy, showing some confusion, but actually open. Rebel sat down carefully beside her friend. "Oh, my God! You're awake!" She picked up Tammy's hand. "How do you feel?"

"I feel like shit. Did somebody drop me off a bridge, run over me a couple times, pick me up and throw me in a closet somewhere?"

"I have no idea. But you have no broken bones, and you're in relatively decent shape, although you've been heavily drugged. However, the drugs are slowly leaving your system."

"Maybe you should tell me what happened." Tammy went to shake her head. Then winced at the movement. "Or maybe not."

"You called me eleven days ago from Daniel's place.

You'd planned to go for the weekend, and that Friday night you called me, you were outraged and said you were on your way home. You said you would call me and talk to me as soon as you got there and that you didn't want anything to do with him. Except," Rebel took a deep breath and added, "you never called me back."

Tammy stared at her in confusion. "Eleven days ago?"

Rebel nodded. "Eleven days ago," she said quietly. "I've been looking for you ever since."

Tammy gently squeezed Rebel's hand. "Thank you for finding me."

"We made a deal with the devil to get you back. Thankfully it worked."

Tammy frowned as she lay in the bed, her face crinkling up with memories. "Daniel was with me?"

Rebel nodded. "We got him too."

"All is well that ends well." She rolled her head from side to side. "It's all so foggy, so distant, as if I can't quite remember."

"And maybe that's a good thing. They kept you sedated so you wouldn't cause any trouble."

"Figures. I remember fighting with Daniel and then being attacked as I left his building." Her eyelids flew open. "It was two men. I remember them injecting me with something."

"Yes, it would make sense to have done so right away. I don't even know if they kept you that way for the whole eleven days, but I'd presume you were awake part of the time."

"We were, part of the time. I remember eating, going to the bathroom. We were allowed to step outside on the deck for a little while. But we couldn't see anything but trees.

Then I was led back inside and tied up again, given more shots." She stared at her arm. "I feel like a pincushion."

"Well, it's over now. You can forget about it. All we need is to get you happy and healthy again."

Tammy stared, shadows in her eyes. "I'm trying to understand what led to this."

"Do you remember finding some information you copied on a USB?"

Tammy's frown deepened.

Rebel pressed on. "Information to do with Samantha and Daniel?"

"Samantha, yes. I asked Daniel about it, but he said he wasn't doing that anymore."

"But he had been?"

Slowly Tammy nodded. "I think so. That's the reason we broke up over a year ago. I thought he was doing something illegal. When he came back to me these last few months, he said he was done with it."

"And then you changed your mind about being with him?"

"Something Samantha said at work, just a couple hours earlier. And I thought he either was having an affair with her or was involved with her in some illegal business venture. At his apartment I accused him of it because Samantha had contacted me. He said they weren't having an affair, and he hadn't had a relationship with her at all. That's why I got so mad because I figured he was lying. I tried to walk away, only to end up"—she motioned with her hand—"like this."

"Well, Samantha's not involved anymore. It appears she was selling company info to the higher of two bidders. She was kidnapped by the one she didn't sell to. He beat her very badly. I was supposed to get you back in trade for the USB

key. Instead we got her, and she died right in front of me."
Rebel's voice dropped from the trauma of the memory. "All I
could think of from that point on was that you would be
found in the same shape."

Tammy just stared at her friend in horror. "They killed
Samantha?" She struggled to sit up, then collapsed back into
the bed. "I had no idea it would be so dangerous. I left the
key in your car because I didn't know what else to do with
it."

Rebel nodded. "And a homeless man had his throat
sliced for no reason other than he was in the wrong place at
wrong time. When we found him, he had your locket in his
shoe."

"I remember being at a warehouse, but I don't know for
how long."

Rebel shook her head. "I haunted Daniel's apartment for
days, thinking he was involved." She frowned. "Was he
kidnapped the same time you were?"

Tammy shrugged. "I didn't see him at the beginning. I
don't remember."

"It's okay. We found texts between Daniel and his
brother while you were missing, but they may not have
actually been sent by Daniel. We think he was taken several
days after you were."

She shrugged. "You'd have to ask Daniel. He just
showed up beside me, but I don't remember when." She
closed her eyes and whispered, "So tired."

"Just rest, Tammy. Just rest."

When her friend fell asleep again, Rebel walked out to
the hallway and quickly sent a text to Saul, explaining
Tammy's confusion.

His reply text came back immediately.

**I'm at the hospital talking with Daniel. I'll come
see you when we're done here.**

With a silly grin on her face, she went back inside the
room and sat next to Tammy. She hoped this was all over for
Tammy, but, just in case, Rebel didn't want to leave her
friend alone for very long.

Another fifteen minutes passed before the door opened,
and Dakota, Merk and Stone walked in. Tammy's eyes flew
open, and Rebel reached out a hand to her friend. Tammy
glanced at the men, then back at Rebel and asked, "Who are
they?"

Saul, the last one in, walked forward and said, "We're
part of the group who found you."

Rebel squeezed Tammy's hand.

"And, for that, you have my greatest thanks," Tammy
said quietly.

The men asked a few questions, but they were more
about her health than about anything that had happened to
her.

She did say, "I'm sorry. Everything seems to be pretty
confused in my head at the moment."

They nodded.

"Chances are it will come back slowly." Saul motioned
to Rebel. "I'd like to talk to you outside for a few minutes."

She hopped to her feet and walked out to the hallway.
"What did Daniel say?"

"Apparently she walked out of his apartment late that
Friday night. Daniel didn't know anything about her
subsequent disappearance other than that she wouldn't
return his calls. When she didn't show up for work, he tried
harder to get a hold of her. He was worried after you raised

such a stink about her being gone. At first he thought she had just disappeared because she was so angry with him. But then he made some inquiries to see what else was going on. Samantha warned him how he better stay out of it or else he'd end up like Tammy. Apparently he disappeared the next day."

"And then Samantha disappeared after that?"

He nodded.

"Was he involved with Samantha at any time, like Tammy thought? Businesswise or personal?"

"Apparently not. He wanted to try again with Tammy and had tried to cut all ties with Samantha and her illegal activities. But, of course, that's not so easy to do."

"Is it over?"

"We'd like to think so. We don't know if anybody else in the company is involved. Chances are good there are others, but that doesn't mean whatever they were doing was illegal. Daniel also explained that he set up the breakfast meeting with his brother knowing that, if he didn't show, his brother would go looking for him."

She nodded. "Good. Hopefully we can move past this now."

Saul looked at her intently for a moment. "What are your plans?"

She grimaced. "While the contents of my apartment are now garbage, I don't have very much in the way of belongings anymore. Nor do I have a place of my own to stay in. Although I could crash at Tammy's apartment, it doesn't have the same comforting feel as it did before." She gazed at him and shrugged. "Aren't you going home now?"

He nodded. "I'll be leaving soon."

She took a deep breath. "Do we get to spend any more

time together?"

"We'll be doing whatever it takes to finalize this job to-day."

"I need to stop in at work to see if I still have a job."

"You may not have a job? Why?"

"I took last week off with vacation pay, but, this week, well, I'm not sure. I talked to HR a couple days ago, but it's not like I said anything about coming back. If I was the boss of the company, I wouldn't hire me back again," she admitted.

He smirked. "You could always move to Texas."

She froze, her heart stalling, her gaze widening. Then she relaxed. "You're just kidding." Inside, her heart started to beat again. How she wished he wasn't kidding. But she wasn't the impulsive type. Okay, not that long-term kind of impulsive anyway. How the hell could she possibly make a move all the way to Texas?

Her mind told her that, if there was a time to make that move, now was it. No possessions, minimal belongings, an insurance check to start over with, a job she probably had to replace anyway.

"But Tammy," she muttered under her breath. "I can't leave her."

Saul grinned. "Bring her. Sounds like she should get away from here after all this too."

"I can't make that decision for her," Rebel said honestly. "And she'll likely need a lot of support for a little while."

"Maybe," Saul said. "But what I also saw was a woman already on the road to recovery."

"Almost. I'm not sure she doesn't have something going on with Daniel. So she may want to stay here to see if the two of them could make their relationship work."

Saul nodded. "You don't want to leave her then, do you?" He stared off in the distance, then seemed to take a mental and a physical step back.

One she instantly hated.

She shook her head. "Tammy'll be here all day, possibly overnight. After that I can always go to her place with her."

"Or you can leave her to get some solid sleep here, and you could come back to Richard's to spend the night with me."

"That sounds appealing too." She pursed her lips thinking about it. "Chances are the doctors will keep her overnight for observation anyway."

Saul nodded. "Exactly. I'll see you in a few hours. The guys and I have things to check up on. We'll be back to look in on Daniel in a bit. I think Foster's planning a big dinner for all of us tonight to celebrate."

She smiled. "That sounds lovely. I'll stay in touch. I have my car, so we'll be good here."

He nodded. "Okay, if you leave here, let me know."

The door to Tammy's hospital room opened, and the other men came out. There was a bit of an awkward silence as she studied them. She quickly took a few steps toward the room and said, "I'll see you later."

Once inside, she sat down, smiling at her friend and gently squeezing her hand.

Tammy studied Rebel with knowing eyes. "I see you found someone you're into."

Rebel's eyebrows rose. "What are you talking about?"

"The man waiting for you. You've been so damn picky for the last couple years that I figured you'd never find anyone. But you knew, didn't you? As soon as you saw him, you knew."

"No, I didn't know right off the bat. And even now I'm not sure. He works in Texas. Only a few months ago he lived here, but he moved to Texas to join the security company he works for now." She stared off in the distance. "He did suggest I move there, though I'm sure he was only joking."

"What's stopping you?"

Rebel stared at her friend, her jaw dropping. "Are you serious? I'm not giving up everything I've got here and leaving you to go to a state where I don't have a job and I don't know anybody."

"We know people. Or have you forgotten the girls we went to school with? They moved to Texas."

"But we haven't seen them in years."

"So?" Tammy asked. "I won't have a problem calling them out of the blue. We talk to them on social media all the time."

Rebel tapped her friend's arm. "That doesn't mean I should just pack up and leave."

"Oh? What do you want to do then? Go back to the same old job?" Tammy stared at her. "I don't know that I want to go back to that job. I sure don't want to work for the same company. I'm not sure I even have a job."

"I was thinking the same thing," Rebel admitted. "I didn't show up for work this week when I was supposed to return from my vacation. I basically walked away to find you."

"I collected proof of illegal activities by company employees. Being a whistleblower doesn't bode well for me keeping my current job, much less getting another one."

The two women stared at each other. "We're a mess."

"But we're alive."

Rebel reached out a hand; Tammy reached back.

"Best friends forever."

"But that doesn't mean best friends without boyfriends," Tammy said.

"Maybe. I'm still not so sure."

"Nobody said you had to be sure. But, in order to find out, you have to get closer in proximity. He came here and found you, but you may have to go there to see if it's real."

Rebel stared at her friend in shock. "That *so* doesn't sound like you."

"No, maybe not, but nothing like being kidnapped and held for eleven days to make you realize how much being safe and living quiet is boring. It doesn't allow you to branch out of your comfort zone and do the things you wish you were doing. So what if we've never been to Texas? We've never been to New Mexico either. If we move to one state, we can start traveling around all the others. We did a lot of that here. We traveled up to Washington, Oregon and down to Baja. But we've never been to Texas."

"*We?*" Rebel asked to be sure.

Tammy shrugged, then said, "Possibly."

"I don't know where in Texas he lives."

She laughed. "I'm sure we can find out with a quick phone call. Who did you say he worked for?"

"Legendary Security. For a guy name Levi and his partner, Ice."

"Let me see your phone."

Rebel pulled her phone from her pocket and handed it over. Within seconds Tammy had the name and contact information of the company up in her hand.

She held it up so Rebel could see it. While Rebel watched, Tammy hit the Dial button. And she handed it back. "Time to make that call."

Rebel snatched the phone from her best friend's hand. "No, wait." But already a woman's voice was on the other end of the phone.

"Legendary Securities. May I help you?"

Rebel took a deep breath. "I think you already have."

The woman snapped, "Explain."

Rebel recapped the last eleven days the best she could. "So you see, my friend Tammy is now alive and well thanks to the men you sent out here for Daniel. And although Daniel's not my favorite person, I'm very glad he's not dead too."

The woman's voice softened. "You must be Rebel."

"Yes, how did you know?"

"My team told me about you. I'm Ice."

"Oh. Which one?" Rebel asked. "Never mind. Don't answer that question."

Ice's chuckle was low and husky. "They all spoke about you, but Saul said the most."

"Oh, I'm glad to hear that," she said, flustered, heat washing over her cheeks.

"I understand your life in California has been uprooted."

"Well, I don't have a job. I don't have an apartment. I don't have much in the way of belongings," she said, "but I do have a best friend who will need some time and effort to heal."

"Well, when you two are ready, come out for a visit. Maybe you'll both find Texas to your liking."

And Ice hung up.

Rebel turned her head and stared at Tammy. "She said whenever we are ready to visit Texas, maybe we'll find it to our liking."

Tammy grinned.

"And apparently Saul spoke to her about me."

"Live up to your name. Be a rebel."

Rebel shook her head. "I went to hell to find you, and I am not losing you now."

Tammy settled back in her bed and said, "Then we will both go. Lord knows I don't want to stay here."

The two women stared at each other in silence. Finally Rebel spoke up. "We were looking for a change a year or so ago, but we never thought we would do something like this for a man."

"But it's not for a man. It's for our future. Besides, these men are heroes. They saved me and Daniel, and that's worth everything. If there's anything I can do to help them in return, I will."

WHEN SAUL RETURNED to Richard's house that night, his nerves had a frayed edginess to them. He'd been surprised to hear himself ask Rebel to move to Texas, but, at the same time, he realized he wasn't joking. He just knew long-distant relationships wouldn't work. And he'd already risked a lot to make the move to Texas, and, now that he'd settled into that new life, he loved it. But he wanted her, and he had no idea how to make this work. Sure, maybe down the road Levi would open up a California office, but Saul couldn't see that happening right now. It just wasn't the time. They didn't have the manpower or the logistics for something like that. It took a lot to set up a new operation in another state. And honestly Saul wasn't ready to leave Texas. It was beautiful. He was thoroughly enjoying the time he had there. But to think Rebel wouldn't be there with him was a wrench to his heart.

"Any word from Ice on Benji?" Foster asked. He busily worked in the kitchen, preparing dinner.

Saul leaned against the doorframe and shook his head. "Not yet. Ice will update him first chance."

Foster nodded. "That would be good. I'm sure this has been eating at him."

"Yes, I suspect so. I understand we'll be in the air heading home by noon tomorrow."

"That sounds good. And Rebel?" Foster asked.

Saul shrugged. "I'm hoping she'll come back here tonight."

"That would be lovely. She's a nice young lady."

"She is fiercely loyal."

"A lot can be said for that. You could do a lot worse."

Saul gave Foster a suspicious look. "But I won't be here long enough to make anything happen."

Foster turned and smiled. "It's already happened. You just have to decide what you want out of it."

"I made a lot of changes to work with Levi and Ice. I'm not about to give that up."

"And maybe you won't need to." Foster didn't say another word.

Saul went upstairs to his room and packed. While there, he grabbed his phone and called Rebel. "Hey, are you still at the hospital?"

"No, I'm at my office. I decided on a quick trip to HR to see what my options are."

His heart sinking, he said, "You were supposed to call me when you left the hospital. But, more important, did you decide to go back to work?"

"I don't want to work here. But I'm not sure if I've been fired or if I have any severance package coming or if I'd have any good references from them," she said. "I need to sit down and figure out my finances. I also owe them an apology." She paused. "I'm just walking into the front door now. It's a bit late, but I'm hoping Roger is still here."

"I'm back at Richard's."

"Oh, I was hoping to be there when you arrived. I should be about half an hour, hopefully not longer." He heard a knock through the phone. "I'll call you back, okay?"

"How long?"

"Give you a shout in ten minutes," she promised. "I'm getting off on the third floor. If I don't answer, come looking for me," she said with a laugh.

He put away his phone and sat down with his laptop. When ten minutes came and went, and she didn't call, he stared at the phone, willing it to ring. He waited a couple more minutes, but still no call came. Finally he picked up the phone, knowing he was being foolish but unable to get rid of the uneasy feeling.

He dialed the number and got no answer. "Damn." He sent her a text.

You okay? Where are you?

And got no response at all. He waited thirty seconds, staring at his phone, then was out of his room, keys in hand, as he bolted downstairs.

Foster was still in the kitchen. "What's up?"

"She's in trouble."

Saul bolted outside to find Stone, Dakota and Merk standing beside the Jeep, talking about one of Richard's cars. They looked up, startled, as he ran past.

"She's in trouble."

Instantly the Jeep filled with men. Saul hopped into the

driver's side, turned on the engine and ripped from the area. He gave them a running commentary as to what the problem was.

"You sure you shouldn't wait five or ten minutes? Not everybody runs on military time."

"I don't like the idea of her going to that office. Just because we know Samantha was involved doesn't mean others weren't as well."

That shut them up.

He pulled into the parking lot and found her car there. He raced around to the front, but the doors were locked.

Shit. He checked his watch. Now thirty minutes has passed since they spoke.

Hearing noises inside, he turned and saw several people walking out just at that moment. He grabbed the door and held it until the crowd walked out, then they slipped inside.

On the third floor he bolted from the elevator, but the hallway was deserted. He ran down one side, looking at name plates. "Rebel, are you here?" he called out.

He tried opening the door that had the name Roger Ginrod on it, only it was locked. A light was on inside, but it wasn't bright.

Nobody answered his heavy knock. He glanced at the other men. Stone already had his lockpick out, and within two seconds he had the door unlocked. Then he pushed it open.

"Hey, who are you, and what are you doing in here?" A tall slim man bolted to his feet in an angry panic. "Get out of here, or I'll call security."

Saul filled the doorway like an avenging angel. "I'm Saul." He glanced around. "And where the hell is my sweetheart?"

The man walked from behind the desk. "I don't know who you're talking about."

Saul shook his head. She was here; he knew it by his gut feeling. A door was off to the side. While the man protested, Saul walked over and flung it open. Rebel was on top of the boardroom table. A needle in her arm. "This asshole drugged her," Saul yelled. He raced over, ripped out the needle and threw it across the room. "Rebel, can you hear me?"

Her eyelids fluttered, and she groaned. He reached down and kissed her. "Rebel, please wake up. Wake up."

Behind him, he could hear Roger protesting. "I'll call the police."

Merk said, "We'll get the police here all right. Don't you worry about that." Already he was dialing 9-1-1, asking for an ambulance and the police.

Roger was still complaining but went silent when Stone said, "Shut up."

Saul glanced back to see Stone standing over Roger, now sitting cowed before the big man. Damn right. Saul would like a few minutes alone with Roger, but Saul had to look after Rebel first. Furiously he growled, "What the hell was worth hurting all these people for?"

When Roger didn't speak, Saul turned, ready to lunge at him.

"The company is applying for new regulatory concessions. Another company wants to take us over at a cheaper price. Proof of wrongdoing will do that."

"So, *money. Greed.* Presumably you're the one behind Tammy's and Daniel's kidnapping. And hired the intruders who came after Rebel at Richard's house." Saul shook his head and stroked Rebel's cheeks.

"We needed the information she had. I didn't know

about the men who killed Samantha."

Saul ignored Roger, picking up Rebel in his arms and walking to the window where the sunlight would fall across her features. He whispered to her, "I don't know how you slipped into my heart like you did, but I can't let you go. Please wake up." He jostled her ever-so-slightly and studied her features. "Wake up, sweetheart. Please wake up."

Her eyelids lifted slowly, and she stared up at him, dazed. She reached for his face only to have her arm fall back against her body. "Drugged."

"I'll look after you. You just fight it off. Try to stay awake." He turned and carried her gently in his arms as he made his way to the outer office. "Where is that ambulance?"

Stone answered. "On their way. And the police will make sure to get to the bottom of this."

Using a tissue, Dakota picked up the needle Saul had flung from her arm. Dakota stuck the evidence under Roger's nose. "Wanna bet your fingerprints are all over this?"

Saul was already out the office door, calling over his shoulder, "I'm not waiting. I'm taking the Jeep and getting Rebel to the hospital."

Dakota spoke up. "I'll drive." Turning to Stone and Merk, Dakota added, "Once the police come for their prisoner, can you taxi to the hospital? Or I'll come back for you two afterward. Let me know."

Carrying her, his feet going as fast as he could make them without causing Rebel further harm, Saul got into the Jeep with Dakota driving them to the hospital.

"You've got it bad, don't you?"

Saul gave a heavy sigh. "Apparently."

"I'm jealous, man. I didn't think you'd find somebody, but, just like that, boom, there she is."

"But is she the right one?"

"From the look of your reaction right now, she has to be."

"That's not fair. Maybe I'd feel this way about any girl-friend."

"No, not like this. You just have to look inside your heart, and then you'll see."

Saul settled back in his seat, holding her close. He had a seat belt on, but she didn't. There wasn't any other way to do it. He didn't dare wait any longer for an ambulance. This was faster.

When they reached the hospital, he unbuckled his seat belt and stepped out with her in his arms. He carried her right into the first empty emergency cubicle and laid her on one of the beds.

The same doctor that had been dealing with Tammy came over, took one look at Saul and asked, "Another one?"

He nodded. "We found the needle this time, and she couldn't have had more than fifteen to twenty minutes alone with the kidnapper."

The doctor took the needle from Dakota and put it in a specimen bag, setting it off to the side, and said, "Step away."

Saul had no choice but to back up while the medical team went to work on Rebel. He paced outside in the waiting room, impatient for the doctor to come out.

When he joined them, he had a smile on his face. "She'll be fine. She's awake, not very cognizant, but she's awake. She keeps calling for Saul."

Saul stepped forward. "That's me."

"Good. We will put her in the same room as her friend."

After that, events happened fast as they moved Rebel on

a gurney to Tammy's room. Tammy took one look at her and cried out. Saul quickly explained about her trip to HR and what had happened.

Tammy stared at him in horror. "That's terrible. She walked right into a trap."

"Either one of you could've done the same thing. The good thing is, this should put an end to that company at least."

"It definitely does for us. We're not going back."

"Good. Then you tell her that she needs to come to Texas."

Tammy chuckled. "We were talking about it earlier. It's one reason she went to see Roger. To see about money owed her and any chance for references."

Saul studied her, hope in his heart. "Really? Would you move with her?"

Dakota walked in just then and stepped up beside Saul. He studied Tammy with interest. "Seriously, would you do that for your friend?"

"Well, we have to pack up my apartment, and I'm still weak. But we'd be willing to make a few months' trial run anyway. I could even put my stuff in storage if we couldn't find a place immediately."

Saul smiled at her. "You're a good friend."

Tammy said slowly, "One of the things you learn in life is that, when you find real friends, you're friends forever. You make compromises for them."

Saul was happy to hear it and nodded in agreement. "Exactly. All of us at Legendary have exactly the same philosophy."

"She'd be very lucky to end up with you," Tammy said sincerely. "And you'd be very blessed to have her."

Saul sat down on the bed beside Rebel. He gently stroked her cheek. "Hey, beauty, wake up now."

Rebel's eyelids fluttered open, but a smile teased at the corner of her mouth. "I knew you'd come."

"How the hell did you know that?" he protested.

"Because you're my hero. That's what heroes do," she whispered, then her eyes drift closed.

He leaned forward and whispered, "This is not exactly how I planned to spend our night together. You know that, right?"

A small chuckle slipped out. "Well, tell the doctor to give me something to push this crap through my veins faster. I have no intention of staying here if the alternative is a night in your arms."

"Or you can move to Texas, and you can spend a lot of nights in my arms."

"Find me a place to live, and you got a deal. If you want me, that is." Just then the drugs took over again, and she slipped into a peaceful sleep.

"But you'll remember what you said when you wake up, right?"

"She will," Tammy said in a serious voice. "She's talked of very little else."

"Good. What kind of accommodations do you two want?"

Tammy smiled and said, "We're not fussy. But I'm in IT, and she's in marketing, so it needs to be some place where we can find related work."

"No problem," Dakota said with a big grin from just inside the doorway. He turned to look at Saul. "Maybe it's time to talk to Ice."

Saul's eyebrows raised as he stared at Dakota. "Really?

You're thinking what I'm thinking?"

"Why not? Even if Legendary doesn't need anybody, I'm sure they know somebody who does."

On that Saul agreed. Maybe he could make his future happen after all, keeping his job and keeping his woman.

A whisper drifted toward him. "Saul?"

He softly rested his hand on Rebel's cheek. "I'm here."

She smiled. "Do you want me to move?"

Her voice was so low that he could barely hear her. He leaned closer and whispered, "I want nothing else but to have you at my side for the rest of my life."

When there was no answer, he figured she'd fallen asleep again.

But her fingers laced with his. "Good. Make it happen."

And she was out for the night this time.

Epilogue

D AKOTA WAITED OUTSIDE, apart from the others who
stood nearby in a group, when the girls finally pulled
up in Saul's Jeep. He grinned when he saw Rebel. She looked
great. He hoped Saul appreciated the steps she'd taken to be
here. Hell, the steps Dakota had taken to reunite Saul with
Rebel … and his Jeep.

She hopped out, ran over and threw her arms around
him. "Is Saul back yet?"

He lifted her up and gave her a big hug. "Anytime now.
They were stuck in Chicago."

"Good. We got here before him." She grinned. "Does he
know I was en route?"

Dakota grinned and said, "Nope, it's a secret."

She rolled her eyes, but they were dancing. "I'm so glad
we could arrange for his Jeep to come with us too. The
moving truck towed it behind, like you said." She grinned.
"But I figured maybe he'd be happy to see it *and* me."

Dakota chuckled. "Oh, I don't think that's an issue."

Tammy got out of the passenger side and walked over.
"Hi, Dakota. Nice to see you again."

Dakota smiled at her, hardly recognizing the woman in
front of him. "Wow, you look so much better now."

"Well, I was kind of drugged the last time you saw me."

"True enough," he said with a smile. "Come on over so I

can introduce you both to the others."

Rebel walked over and introduced herself to the nearby group. Levi took one look at Rebel and smiled. "So you're Saul's sweetheart, are you?"

She shrugged. "Not so sure about that, but he's definitely my hunky hero."

At the grimace that crossed Levi's face, and the chuckle that came from the woman by his side, Rebel added, "If it wasn't for him, I wouldn't have made it here today."

Ice spoke up. "Levi's not fond of being called a hero. Most of the guys are the same."

Rebel shook her head, addressing the men in the group. "You need to just accept the fact that you guys are all heroes. It doesn't matter what the circumstances are, you all step up and take care of business, and I for one appreciate that." She glanced around the faces and said, "And I thank you for my life."

Tammy stood beside her best friend. "Thank you for mine as well."

Ice smiled at the two women. "You're very welcome. Come on in and get some coffee."

The women headed inside, leaving some of the men straggling behind.

Levi glared at Dakota. "Did you tell her about the heroes stuff?"

Dakota chuckled. "No, but Saul might've. They've been on the phone steadily since we left them behind, although I think you deliberately tried to keep him away from her."

Levi shrugged. "I had to keep his mind busy. He was constantly distracted," he muttered.

"Maybe for a good reason," Dakota said.

A small truck hurtled into the compound. Saul hopped

from the driver's seat, his gaze freezing at the sight of his Jeep. "Where is she?" he roared.

Hearing Saul's voice, Rebel slammed through the back door as she raced past Dakota and threw herself into Saul's arms.

It was almost embarrassing to see the two of them, lost for so long and now found.

And yet, so heartwarming and loving.

Dakota gave a happy sigh for his friend and Rebel, now united again.

"This is getting ridiculous," Levi said. "I feel like I'm running a matchmaking center here."

Ice walked over to join Levi and Dakota with a big grin on her face. "If you are, you're doing a damn fine job of it." She patted Dakota on the shoulder. "Not to worry, we'll find somebody for you too."

He shook his head and held up his hands. "No way. I'm good. The single life suits me just fine."

Levi wrapped an arm around Ice, held her close and whispered, "He just doesn't get it yet, does he?"

Ice smiled up at Levi, the love of her life, and said, "No, but he will."

This concludes Book 8 of Heroes for Hire: Saul's Sweetheart.

Read about Dakota's Delight: Heroes for Hire, Book 9

Heroes for Hire: Dakota's Delight (Book #9)

Recovering from the loss of her husband hasn't been easy for Bailey, and she's retreated from life to the point where she goes to work, comes home, and that's the most she can say she's done every day...that is, until one morning she walks into the place she works and witnesses a murder.

Terrified she'll be next, she flees into traffic and nearly gets run over. What might have been her death instead awakens the spark of life inside her again. Just as ironically, the man driving the car that almost hit her awakens another ache she'd assumed was forever gone with her husband.

Dakota persuades her to move into the compound where he's employed, Legendary Securities, for her own safety. With his promise to track down the murderer she'd witnessed, Bailey has no choice but to accept the help. Before long, it's no longer her life she's most worried about losing. Will the man who almost ran her down steal her heart?

Book 9 is available now!

To find out more visit Dale Mayer's website.

https://geni.us/DMDakotauniversal

Other Military Series by Dale Mayer

SEALs of Honor

Heroes for Hire

SEALs of Steel

The K9 Files

The Mavericks

Bullards Battle

Hathaway House

Terkel's Team

Ryland's Reach: Bullard's Battle (Book #1)

Welcome to a new stand-alone but interconnected series from Dale Mayer. This is Bullard's story—and that of his team's. All raw, rough, incredibly capable men who have one goal: to find out who was behind the attack on their leader, before the attacker, or attackers, return to finish the job.

Stay tuned for more nonstop action as the men narrow down their suspects ... and find a way to let love back into their own empty lives.

His rescue from the ocean after a horrible plane explosion was his top priority, in any way, shape, or form. A small sailboat and a nurse to do the job was more than Ryland hoped for.

When Tabi somehow drags him and his buddy Garret onboard and surprisingly gets them to a naval ship close by, Ryland figures he'd used up all his luck and his friend's too. Sure enough, those who attacked the plane they were in weren't content to let him slowly die in the ocean. No. Surviving had made him a target all over again.

Tabi isn't expecting her sailing holiday to include the rescue of two badly injured men and then to end with the loss of her beloved sailboat. Her instincts save them, but now she finds it tough to let them go—even as more of Bullard's team members come to them—until it becomes apparent that not only are Bullard and his men still targets … but she is too.

BULLARD CHECKED THAT the helicopter was loaded with their bags and that his men were ready to leave.

He walked back one more time, his gaze on Ice. She'd never looked happier, never looked more perfect. His heart ached, but he knew she remained a caring friend and always would be. He opened his arms; she ran into them, and he held her close, whispering, "The offer still stands."

She leaned back and smiled up at him. "Maybe if and when Levi's been gone for a long enough time for me to forget," she said in all seriousness.

"That's not happening. You two, now three, will live long and happy lives together," he said, smiling down at the woman knew to be the most beautiful, inside and out. She would never be his, but he always kept a little corner of his heart open and available, in case she wanted to surprise him and to slide inside.

And then he realized she'd already been a part of his heart all this time. That was a good ten to fifteen years by now. But she kept herself in the friend category, and he understood because she and Levi, partners and now parents, were perfect together.

Bullard reached out and shook Levi's hand. "It was a hell of a blast," he said. "When you guys do a big splash, you really do a *big* splash."

Ice laughed. "A few days at home sounds perfect for me now."

"It looks great," he said, his hands on his hips as he surveyed the people in the massive pool surrounded by the palm trees, all designed and decked out by Ice. Right beside all the war machines that he heartily approved of. He grinned at her. "When are you coming over to visit?" His gaze went to Levi, raising his eyebrows back at her. "You guys should come over for a week or two or three."

"It's not a bad idea," Levi said. "We could use a long holiday, just not yet."

"That sounds familiar." Bullard grinned. "Anyway, I'm off. We'll hit the airport and then pick up the plane and head home." He added, "As always, call if you need me."

Everybody raised a hand as he returned to the helicopter and his buddy who was flying him to the airport. Ice had volunteered to shuttle him there, but he hadn't wanted to take her away from her family or to prolong the goodbye. He hopped inside, waving at everybody as the helicopter lifted. Two of his men, Ryland and Garret, were in the back seats. They always traveled with him.

Bullard would pick up the rest of his men in Australia. He stared down at the compound as he flew overhead. He preferred his compound at home, but damn they'd done a nice job here.

With everybody on the ground screaming goodbye, Bullard sailed over Houston, heading toward the airport. His two men never said a word. They all knew how he felt about Ice. But not one of them would cross that line and say anything. At least not if they expected to still have jobs.

It was one thing to fall in love with another man's woman, but another thing to fall in love with a woman who was so unique, so different, and so absolutely perfect that you knew, just knew, there was no hope of finding anybody else like her. But she and Levi had been together way before Bullard had ever met her, which made it that much more heartbreaking.

Still, he'd turned and looked forward. He had a full roster of jobs himself to focus on when he got home. Part of him was tired of the life; another part of him couldn't wait to head out on the next adventure. He managed to run everything from his command centers in one or two of his locations. He'd spent a lot of time and effort at the second one and kept a full team at both locations, yet preferred to spend most of his time at the old one. It felt more like home to him, and he'd like to be there now, but still had many more days before that could happen.

The helicopter lowered to the tarmac, he stepped out, said his goodbyes and walked across to where his private plane waited. It was one of the things that he loved, being a pilot of both helicopters and airplanes, and owning both birds himself.

That again was another way he and Ice were part of the same team, of the same mind-set. He'd been looking for another woman like Ice for himself, but no such luck. Sure, lots were around for short-term relationships, but most of them couldn't handle his lifestyle or the violence of the world that he lived in. He understood that.

The ones who did had a hard edge to them that he found difficult to live with. Bullard appreciated everybody's being alert and aware, but if there wasn't some softness in the women, they seemed to turn cold all the way through.

As he boarded his small plane, Ryland and Garret following behind, Bullard called out in his loud voice, "Let's go, slow pokes. We've got a long flight ahead of us."

The men grinned, confident Bullard was teasing, as was his usual routine during their off-hours.

"Well, we're ready, not sure about you though ..." Ryland said, smirking.

"We're waiting on you this time," Garret added with a chuckle. "Good thing you're the boss."

Bullard grinned at his two right-hand men. "Isn't that the truth?" He dropped his bags at one of the guys' feet and said, "Stow all this stuff, will you? I want to get our flight path cleared and get the hell out of here."

They'd all enjoyed the break. He tried to get over once a year to visit Ice and Levi and same in reverse. But it was time to get back to business. He started up the engines, got confirmation from the tower. They were heading to Australia for this next job. He really wanted to go straight back to Africa, but it would be a while yet. They'd refuel in Honolulu.

Ryland came in and sat down in the copilot's spot, buckled in, then asked, "You ready?"

Bullard laughed. "When have you ever known me *not* to be ready?" At that, he taxied down the runway. Before long he was up in the air, at cruising level, and heading to Hawaii. "Gotta love these views from up here," Bullard said. "This place is magical."

"It is once you get up above all the smog," he said. "Why Australia again?"

"Remember how we were supposed to check out that newest compound in Australia that I've had my eye on? Besides the alpha team is coming off that ugly job in Sydney. We'll give them a day or two of R&R then head home."

"Right. We could have some equally ugly payback on that job."

Bullard shrugged. "That goes for most of our jobs. It's the life."

"And don't you have enough compounds to look after?"

"Yes I do, but that kid in me still looks to take over the world. Just remember that."

"Better you go home to Africa and look after your first two compounds," Ryland said.

"Maybe," Bullard admitted. "But it seems hard to not continue expanding."

"You need a partner," Ryland said abruptly. "That might ease the savage beast inside. Keep you home more."

"Well, the only one I like," he said, "is married to my best friend."

"I'm sorry about that," Ryland said quietly. "What a shit deal."

"No," Bullard said. "I came on the scene last. They were always meant to be together. Especially now they are a family."

"If you say so," Ryland said.

Bullard nodded. "Damn right, I say so."

And that set the tone for the next many hours. They landed in Hawaii, and while they fueled up everybody got off to stretch their legs by walking around outside a bit as this was a small private airstrip, not exactly full of hangars and tourists. Then they hopped back on board again for takeoff.

"I can fly," Ryland offered as they took off.

"We'll switch in a bit," Bullard said. "Surprisingly, I'm doing okay yet, but I'll let you take her down."

"Yeah, it's still a long flight," Ryland said studying the islands below. It was a stunning view of the area.

"I love the islands here. Sometimes I just wonder about the benefit of, you know, crashing into the sea, coming up on a deserted island, and finding the simple life again," Bullard said with a laugh.

"I hear you," Ryland said. "Every once in a while, I wonder the same."

Several hours later Ryland looked up and said abruptly, "We've made good time considering we've already passed Fiji."

Bullard yawned.

"Let's switch."

Bullard smiled, nodded, and said, "Fine. I'll hand it over to you."

Just then a funny noise came from the engine on the right side.

They looked at each other, and Ryland said, "Uh-oh. That's not good news."

Boom!

And the plane exploded.

Find Bullard's Battle (Book #1) here!

To find out more visit Dale Mayer's website.

https://geni.us/DMRylandUniversal

Damon's Deal: Terkel's Team (Book #1)

Welcome to a brand-new connected series of intrigue, betrayal, and ... murder, from the *USA Today* best-selling author Dale Mayer. A series with all the elements you've come to love, plus so much more... including psychics!

A betrayal from within has Terkel frantic to protect those he can, as his team falls one by one, from a murderous killer he helped create.

ICE POURED HERSELF a coffee and sat down at the compound's massive dining room table with the others. When her phone rang, she smiled at the number displayed. "Hey, Terk. How're you doing?" She put the call on Speakerphone.

"I'm okay," Terkel said, his voice distracted and tight.

"Terk?" Merk called from across the table. He got up and walked closer and sat across from Levi. "You don't sound too good, brother. What's up?"

"I'm fine," Terk said. "Or I will be. Right now, things are blown to shit."

"As in literally?" Merk asked.

"The entire group," Terk said, "they're all gone. I had a solid team of eight, and they're all gone."

"Dead?"

Several others stood to join them, gathered around Ice's phone. Levi stepped forward, his hand on Ice's shoulder. "Terk? Are they all dead?"

"No." Terk took a deep breath. "I'm not making sense. I'm sorry."

"Take it easy," Ice said, her voice calm and reassuring. "What do you mean, *they're all gone?*"

"All their abilities are gone," he said. "Something's happened to them. Somebody has deliberately removed whatever super senses they could utilize—or what we have been utilizing for the last ten years for the government." His tone was bitter. "When the US gov recently closed us down, they promised that our black ops department would never rise again, but I didn't expect them to attack us personally."

"What are you talking about?" Merk said in alarm, standing up now to stare at Ice's phone. "Are you in danger?"

"Maybe? I don't know," Terk said. "I need to find out exactly what the hell's going on."

"What can we do to help?" Ice asked.

Terk gave a broken laugh. "That's not why I'm calling. Well, it is, but it isn't."

Ice looked at Merk, who frowned, as he shook his head. Ice knew he and the others had heard Terk's stressed out tone and the completely confusing bits and pieces coming from his mouth. Ice said, "Terk, you're not making sense again. Take a breath and explain. Please. You're scaring me."

Terk took a long slow deep breath. "Tell Stone to open the gate," he said. "She's out there."

"Who's out there?" Levi asked, hopped up, looked outside, and shrugged.

"She's coming up the road now. You have to let her in."

"Who? Why?"

"*Because*," he said, "she's also harnessed with C-4."

"Jesus," Levi said, bolting to display the camera feeds to the big screen in the room. "Is it live?"

"It is, and she's been sent to you."

"Well, that's an interesting move," Ice said, her voice sharp, activating her comm to connect to Stone in the control room. "Who's after us?"

"I think it's rebels within the Iranian government. But it could be our own government. I don't know anymore," Terk snapped. "I also don't know how they got her so close to you. Or how they pinned your connection to me," he said. "I've been very careful."

"We can look after ourselves," Ice said immediately. "But who is this woman to you?"

"She's pregnant," he said, "so that adds to the intensity here."

"Understood. So who is the father? Is he connected somehow?"

There was silence on the other end.

Merk said, "Terk, talk to us."

"She's carrying my baby," Terk replied, his voice heavy.

Merk, his expression grim, looked at Ice, her face mirroring his shock. He asked, "How do you know her, Terk?"

"Brother, you don't understand," Terk said. "I've never met this woman before in my life." And, with that, the phone went dead.

Find Terkel's Team (Book #1) here!

To find out more visit Dale Mayer's website.

https://geni.us/DMTTDamonUniversal

Author's Note

Thank you for reading Saul's Sweetheart: Heroes for Hire, Book 8! If you enjoyed the book, please take a moment and leave a short review.

Dear reader,

I love to hear from readers, and you can contact me at my website: www.dalemayer.com or at my Facebook author page. To be informed of new releases and special offers, sign up for my newsletter or follow me on BookBub. And if you are interested in joining Dale Mayer's Reader Group, here is the Facebook sign up page.
http://geni.us/DaleMayerFBGroup

Cheers,
Dale Mayer

About the Author

Dale Mayer is a *USA Today* best-selling author, best known for her SEALs military romances, her Psychic Visions series, and her Lovely Lethal Garden cozy series. Her contemporary romances are raw and full of passion and emotion (Broken But ... Mending, Hathaway House series). Her thrillers will keep you guessing (Kate Morgan, By Death series), and her romantic comedies will keep you giggling (*It's a Dog's Life*, a stand-alone novella; and the Broken Protocols series, starring Charming Marvin, the cat).

Dale honors the stories that come to her—and some of them are crazy, break all the rules and cross multiple genres!

To go with her fiction, she also writes nonfiction in many different fields, with books available on résumé writing, companion gardening, and the US mortgage system. All her books are available in print and ebook format.

Connect with Dale Mayer Online

Dale's Website – www.dalemayer.com
Twitter – @DaleMayer
Facebook Page – geni.us/DaleMayerFBFanPage
Facebook Group – geni.us/DaleMayerFBGroup
BookBub – geni.us/DaleMayerBookbub
Instagram – geni.us/DaleMayerInstagram
Goodreads – geni.us/DaleMayerGoodreads
Newsletter – geni.us/DaleNews

Also by Dale Mayer

Published Adult Books:

Bullard's Battle
Ryland's Reach, Book 1
Cain's Cross, Book 2
Eton's Escape, Book 3
Garret's Gambit, Book 4
Kano's Keep, Book 5
Fallon's Flaw, Book 6
Quinn's Quest, Book 7
Bullard's Beauty, Book 8
Bullard's Best, Book 9

Terkel's Team
Damon's Deal, Book 1

Kate Morgan
Simon Says… Hide, Book 1

Hathaway House
Aaron, Book 1
Brock, Book 2
Cole, Book 3
Denton, Book 4

Elliot, Book 5

Finn, Book 6

Gregory, Book 7

Heath, Book 8

Iain, Book 9

Jaden, Book 10

Keith, Book 11

Lance, Book 12

Melissa, Book 13

Nash, Book 14

Owen, Book 15

Hathaway House, Books 1–3

Hathaway House, Books 4–6

Hathaway House, Books 7–9

The K9 Files

Ethan, Book 1

Pierce, Book 2

Zane, Book 3

Blaze, Book 4

Lucas, Book 5

Parker, Book 6

Carter, Book 7

Weston, Book 8

Greyson, Book 9

Rowan, Book 10

Caleb, Book 11

Kurt, Book 12

Tucker, Book 13

Harley, Book 14

The K9 Files, Books 1–2

The K9 Files, Books 3–4

The K9 Files, Books 5–6

The K9 Files, Books 7–8

The K9 Files, Books 9–10

The K9 Files, Books 11–12

Lovely Lethal Gardens

Arsenic in the Azaleas, Book 1

Bones in the Begonias, Book 2

Corpse in the Carnations, Book 3

Daggers in the Dahlias, Book 4

Evidence in the Echinacea, Book 5

Footprints in the Ferns, Book 6

Gun in the Gardenias, Book 7

Handcuffs in the Heather, Book 8

Ice Pick in the Ivy, Book 9

Jewels in the Juniper, Book 10

Killer in the Kiwis, Book 11

Lifeless in the Lilies, Book 12

Murder in the Marigolds, Book 13

Lovely Lethal Gardens, Books 1–2

Lovely Lethal Gardens, Books 3–4

Lovely Lethal Gardens, Books 5–6

Lovely Lethal Gardens, Books 7–8

Lovely Lethal Gardens, Books 9–10

Psychic Vision Series

Tuesday's Child

Hide 'n Go Seek

Maddy's Floor

Garden of Sorrow

Knock Knock…

Rare Find

Eyes to the Soul

Now You See Her

Shattered

Into the Abyss

Seeds of Malice

Eye of the Falcon

Itsy-Bitsy Spider

Unmasked

Deep Beneath

From the Ashes

Stroke of Death

Ice Maiden

Snap, Crackle…

Psychic Visions Books 1–3

Psychic Visions Books 4–6

Psychic Visions Books 7–9

By Death Series

Touched by Death

Haunted by Death

Chilled by Death

By Death Books 1–3

Broken Protocols – Romantic Comedy Series

Cat's Meow

Cat's Pajamas

Cat's Cradle

Cat's Claus

Broken Protocols 1-4

Broken and... Mending

Skin

Scars

Scales (of Justice)

Broken but... Mending 1-3

Glory

Genesis

Tori

Celeste

Glory Trilogy

Biker Blues

Morgan: Biker Blues, Volume 1

Cash: Biker Blues, Volume 2

SEALs of Honor

Mason: SEALs of Honor, Book 1

Hawk: SEALs of Honor, Book 2

Dane: SEALs of Honor, Book 3

Swede: SEALs of Honor, Book 4

Shadow: SEALs of Honor, Book 5

Cooper: SEALs of Honor, Book 6

Heroes for Hire

Shane, Book 12

Diesel, Book 13

Jerricho, Book 14

The Mavericks, Books 1–2

The Mavericks, Books 3–4

The Mavericks, Books 5–6

The Mavericks, Books 7–8

The Mavericks, Books 9–10

The Mavericks, Books 11–12

Collections

Dare to Be You...

Dare to Love...

Dare to be Strong...

RomanceX3

Standalone Novellas

It's a Dog's Life

Riana's Revenge

Second Chances

Published Young Adult Books:

Family Blood Ties Series

Vampire in Denial

Vampire in Distress

Vampire in Design

Vampire in Deceit

Vampire in Defiance

Vampire in Conflict

Vampire in Chaos

Vampire in Crisis

Vampire in Control

Vampire in Charge

Family Blood Ties Set 1–3

Family Blood Ties Set 1–5

Family Blood Ties Set 4–6

Family Blood Ties Set 7–9

Sian's Solution, A Family Blood Ties Series Prequel
 Novelette

Design series

Dangerous Designs

Deadly Designs

Darkest Designs

Design Series Trilogy

Standalone

In Cassie's Corner

Gem Stone (a Gemma Stone Mystery)

Time Thieves

Published Non-Fiction Books:

Career Essentials

Career Essentials: The Résumé

Career Essentials: The Cover Letter

Career Essentials: The Interview

Career Essentials: 3 in 1